Tyrannos

X

Basileus

Baylen James

Twin Path Press

To those in search of a better life, might death aid in your discovery.

January 13

x It is not unlike him to be missing for days at a time. I do not go searching for him. If I call and he comes to me, I know he is around. If he does not, then he could be anywhere, most often not here.

x Why does music play everywhere one goes, is sound unlike the other senses? Does sound require that one listens? If one wants to see they cannot close their eyes, if one wants to breathe they must smell, to eat they must taste, but to hear, one does not only hear through their ears, can you truly disengage, can one deny sound? A thing that one must feel and hear? Vibrations, felt through touch, heard by one's ears; one must always touch the ground, whether indirectly or through one's own bones and the skin which wraps around them. I quite dislike sound.

x Sitting on this chair I watch them. I do not enjoy doing much myself, I tire easily and at the faintest inconvenience I feel the rage of my ancestors well in my chest, so I do not do much. Trevor is my favorite, he works quick and efficient but his drinks taste the same if not better than that one girl, her name always escapes me, but Trevor, how could one forget him? He's quite kind and talks to everyone in a way that makes you think he cares, he may even, though I am doubtful of

1

motives beyond the necessary. When he speaks to me I feel as if I have a friend - I have few friends and choose not to engage others, so please do not feel bad for me - a friend that knows who I am despite his knowledge being limited to my name and favorite drink order. I know little about him too, but I watch. Watching is almost as good as knowing, you can see more in someone by observing their face than listening to their chatter. No one speaks the truth, most people are unable to find it within them even if they wanted to talk with true intention, so I watch.

"I think we should go to Maladi."

"Hm. When?"

"March. I checked and there's two weeks we have off together."

"I was planning on seeing my mother."

"Aren't you off this weekend?"

"I don't feel like it."

"I know. But I think it would be good for us. Get out before our nine months straight."

"Nine months."

"Exactly."

"I'll think about it."

"Please."

"Fine."

"I'll take care of everything, just meet me at the airport on the ninth."

"Can I ride with you?"

He smiled, "Sure, I'll pick you up in the morning then?"

"Okay."

"Ah! I'm excited."

"Nine months

x I had dreams once. I sometimes still do dream, not as much as

2

when I was a child albeit, but they still exist. When I was younger I dreamt of being apart of a secret military group fighting aliens, or becoming a knight in a feudal civilization, or sailing the seas as a lackey to the grand pirate king. Now I have simple dreams, seeing the mountains of Nepal, living on a plot larger than ten acres and waking up to see the stars setting and the wind blowing the trees in my backyard, and being happy are among them. These are my "dreams", I am not sure if they're truly what I want, or what I have settled for after looking to the past and seeing the future will be more of the same. One grandiose dream remains, one of being the ruler, of driving the force of change, having the people rally around me and carrying us into a new generation bringing paradise for all who live and will ever live - a dream of power. The power to make everything alright, to help everyone, to free myself, to be the king. I want to be powerful so badly, for I am not. I wish to use that power for good, for what I think is good. I believe my childhood fantasies brewed something in me and now my last fantasy, the one that will either kill me or stay with me until the day I die, is just a sliver of who I used to be. I want to believe this dream of power will bring me back, if I can only somehow achieve it I can be whole again, I can be joyful and spontaneous and free. But only a fool reaches for the sky and claims his legs are not chained to the earth.

March 9

The plane ride was bumpy. It felt like riding the waves of the ocean in a row boat, something too small to take on nature that big. I hadn't been on a plane since I was a child. Once when I was fourteen, maybe fifteen, I rode to Spain with my grandmother. She had a house there, a nice, quaint house on a cliff facing the coast of Valencia, the water was so blue, the beach an unbelievable white, and the air, there's something about the air anywhere but home. I can smell it here, in the city outside Maladi. I think it's open air, air that comes from somewhere, blowing in with purpose as its wheels and essence as the driver. It's when I breathe in that air that I feel like I might one day know myself, it fills my lungs with a fire that broils my heart. I felt it then because I knew I wanted to escape my home, Spain was good, I wanted to be there forever; and I feel it now for the same reason, Drew brought me here for a momentary relief, two weeks away from everything, away from anywhere, before I have to return to my "life".

"You feeling any better?"

"Than what?"

"Than before we left."

"Well of course, I feel great already." I smile and put my hand on his shoulder.

"Perfect. When we get down there you'll understand why I come every chance I get."

"How often is that?"

"Twice a year if I'm lucky."

"Maybe I'll start coming with you."

"I'd love it if you did," I'd love it if I could, "it gets lonely in Maladi."

"Is it really that far down?"

"Yep! Once we leave there's no coming back until we're ready to come home."

"What if something happens, we get hurt or

"Then you die!" My stomach weighs a thousand pounds. He shoves me. "I'm joking of course, never had that happen but I think we could get a doctor or something I don't know."

"Are all these people here just for us?"

"Yes and no, they came for us today yes but this is what they do, they work for the adventure."

"For our adventure."

He shakes his head, "You'll see."

"Is that why we can't leave at night?"

"That and it's dark, can't see if there's no sun." I notice now that there are no lights, just the setting sun and the occasional flame on a stick or in a lamp.

"So what time should I be ready?"

He laughs at me, loudly. "We leave at first light."

"I better get to bed then."

The edge of the city is bustling. I sit at the front of my tent, staring out at the party gathering supplies and loading everything onto carts, they are more like platforms actually, Drew says they attach to a rail system powered by the river in Maladi which slowly lowers or raises them alongside the trail. We must escort the supplies and the party escorts us, it's a whole system he says. I see they have a system for their preparation too. Each has a different color arm band and so far I have only determined the meaning of the red and yellow ones. There must be at least ten colors but I would need to see them all together, maybe tomorrow I will. Tomorrow, not in the morning or at eight, but tomorrow. I like that about this place, they seem to be having a great time. I need to relax, that's my issue, even here, on vacation in the most relaxing place in the world I cannot bring myself to stop thinking, to stop my mind from racing. Sometimes I feel as if I must tear my skin off, ripping it with my nails, and others I feel simple intrigue at the things around me. I like to think but I do not like that I must think.

The blue. The blue bands are in charge of tools, they have bags full of metallic objects and I can hear them clanging around from here. Why would we possibly need that many tools? I must admit I am rather fascinated by this whole ordeal, the travel party, the manner of descent, the basin itself, this elusive, somewhat mystical if you ask Drew, Maladi. I feel like I traveled into a place where everyone acts as if the rest of the world doesn't exist, we are here now and that is all. I looked over the edge earlier, you can see plenty of thick trunked trees and the ground is covered in greenery and rough, veiny vines, and you can feel that breeze. It comes from somewhere deep in the basin, I can smell water down there too, water like it has been raining not like a lake or the ocean. Water. Plants. But no animals. I did not see a soul and Drew mentioned it once, nothing strays from the path. We must not stray from the path.

March 10

Facing Death, that inescapable journey,
who can be wiser than he
who reflects, while breath yet remains,
on whether his life brought others happiness, or pains,
since his soul may yet win delight's or night's way
after his death-day
-The Venerable Bede or Anonymous

Everyone is laughing and so I laugh too, smiling at the woman I assume has been assigned to guide me. Bearing no arm band, she wields a hatchet, as do all the members of the party, to cut down these Maladian vines. They're unlike any I have ever seen, bulging and thick and writhing and quick, they seem to leap out at us, aiming for a kill with every strike. Someone said they can pierce steel with their tips, another said they could crush an oak tree in half, though I am not sure what to believe, many myths exist surrounding this place it seems. But, the vines appear precarious, one wrong step and you tumble down the slope or get your head taken off by the low hanging ones, and gross. I do not like how they pulsate, and slither like they know where they are, like they can see or sense our passing. And so the vines are chopped down with the hatchets. My guide has other equipment though, clearly visible on her hip is a long blade, most likely around ten inches or so, and another on her ankle of half the size. I noticed when she turned to slice a vine on our left that she concealed another weapon on the inside of her shorts just below the waist, a gun, a small one but it was definitely a gun. The party all seem relaxed. They joke and sing and dance and talk, like all of this is second nature, yet I know there is danger in this journey, I know it now. They would not be ready for it if there was not a chance. But where?

"My friend, we travel together but I do not know your name." A hand on my shoulder.

"Oh, I'm sorry."

"I didn't mean to startle you." He smiles, a joyful people, he pats my back roughly.

"I've just never been to a place like this."

"Ah.. I remember my first trip to Maladi."

"Really?" I act intrigued, he's rambunctious clearly.

"Yes, oh yes. Many years ago when I was young and still brave I came to the city with my older brother Daldrec, the people of our land have been traveling to Maladi since before counted time, but this was only his third trip. He was far more reckless than I if you can imagine that," a sarcastic laugh came from the woman walking beside me, she's playing into his story, "yet he was put in charge of the scouting detail, a very important job back then, when the woods were void of peace. It being my first trip, I was left to escort the cargo like them over there," he pointed to the ones called Lila and Nestor, "so we set out in the spring, early in the day like always, and everything was fine. But the third day, that's when everything went wrong. Daldrec and his scouts didn't come back, for a few hours we thought maybe they'd gotten lost, there's no paths in the deep woods, only trees and trees and more trees, so we sent two more of our best, only they didn't return either. By nightfall the temperature had dropped severely, it was like death himself was breathing on us, I huddled under all the wools I brought, laid next to the bonfire we built, curled next to my brothers and sisters, yet I could feel the cool air in my skin, I could feel it in my pores, even the backs of my eyes were cold. A few died from shock or hypothermia or just being too damn cold, but I survived. And when I awoke, the sun did not rise and the fire was out. It was pure darkness, I couldn't even see my fingers in front of my face, but I could hear. I heard every bit of the ambush, I could hear the tearing of muscle, the resistance in the skin but it tore too, the crushing of bones under loud crashes, it sounded like stepping on a handful of nuts, peanuts with thick shells, I heard screams, and calls for help. But I couldn't find anything except the platform, so I started it up and rode all the way down, never leaving the platform, I couldn't, I didn't sleep for the couple days it took to reach the bottom, staring into the darkness the whole time," he paused for a very long time, I almost thought that was it, he was going to leave the story at that, but when he continued I knew it was part of the story, a long, brooding pause, "when I got to the bottom I learned why they risk their life to reach Maladi, it's something you can't explain with words, but I would sacrifice my own life if it meant I could only go once."

"I don't get it."

"Of course you don't," he seems genuinely offended, "just wait, and trust me." He puts his hand out for me to shake, "I'm Maude."

"It's nice to meet you."

The sun is setting now. In just under an hour we would need to set up camp, the first camp of the trip. I have been tasked with setting up our tent while she searches for wood and other supplies to furnish our living space, and I am uncertain I will be able to do so, I have never been camping before, much less survive in the wilderness, alone. We sleep in pairs so I am not completely alone, but I do not know her, I've yet to learn her name; though it seems she doesn't talk much, so it is of no fault of my own. Even with her protection I feel an ache in my abdomen, a twisting, sharp pain, what if I cannot survive through the night? In Maladi every person fights for their own survival. Would she abandon me even if I am her task? How bound are the party members to the mission, would Maude and the other fighters leave us behind? Never have I wielded a weapon, nor do I have access to one, but would I be able to?

"you don't need to worry about what maude said you know"
"What?" I did not think she would say a word to me the entire trip.
"i can tell you're worried'
"Well yes, but it's not because of Maude." I am clearly lying.
She smiles knowingly, one that crept up on her face, "then what is it"
"What's your name?"
"cynthia"
I nod, "I guess I'm just new to the whole survive or die thing."
"isn't that what survival means"
"Yes... more specifically I've never had to think about it before."
"so the risk of death"
"Yea"
"you risk dying every minute that you live"
I have no response. I wait a few strides down the slope, "Why do you have so many weapons?"
"risk"

I can tell our conversation is over. I turn to my right and see Lila laying on one of the platforms, Nestor walking alongside it. Drew is on the far side with his guide, someone named Ines or Inge or Ina I cannot recall. Maude is nowhere to be seen now, but I presume it is due to his duty to secure the campsite, they must have gone ahead after we finished talking. Everyone is spread out now, separating into their groups for rest, pairs of two, I thought the party was larger but in this setting and under the camp rules we seem sparse, loosely related.

"Cynthia," I turn back to my left but she has already started treading into the wood. She acts as if my voice is faint, only turning her head slightly and giving a quiet call.

"the sun is setting," she yelled this time, loudly, "get us set up or i'll kill you," and she jogged out of sight.

She returned very late, it's hard to tell with the thick bunches of branches and their massive leaves, but it must be almost halfway through the night. I managed to arrange the tent against an outcrop with a steep enough slope to act as a wall, albeit with the assistance of Nestor - I think he has taken a liking to me, kind of like the older brother I wish I had - so that the entire ordeal only took an hour or so as we needed to ensure but two sides of the tent were properly fixed. The rest came easily, everything was prepared hours ago and I sat here waiting. I watched as everyone ate and sat around the fires, I watched as they enjoyed themselves, laughing, carefree. Drew was somewhere among them, I heard his group had joined all their tents and were ready for sleep just after we stopped the platforms. At what point does one become a native of this land? Why is he so easily accepted?

All the lights were out now and the only sound came from the wind rushing through the greenery, rustling the tent flaps, causing the platforms to creak. I still lay outside the tent, I never moved except to accept her return. I did my half, now she must do hers. It is taking her a long time, who knows how long, but I feel like I have been staring into the darkness above for days on end, thinking about everything and nothing at the same time. My brain is tired, this has been a long journey and we're not yet a third of the way through. What have I gotten myself into.

"are you coming in", her voice came from the void, sounded like it belonged there.

"I thought it might be a while," I turn my head in her direction, the light from inside the tent casts a flickering shadow across her face, creeping from the back of her neck to her eyes. Her features are distinct under this light, menacing almost.

"come eat so we can sleep", I nod and pick myself up, ripping myself from the ground which beckons for me.

"The rest have already been asleep."

"okay"

I sit on my bedroll across from her, eating from the bowl which she gave me. It is bland. I think of something to say but I do not speak, she would not respond anyway. She found herself a harsher mood than the one she had all day, so I finish eating and quench the light by my bed. Laying down now I think I like the feeling of the earth below me more than the thin sheet and underside of the tent. The artificial nature of such things deter real engagement, I feel detached from where I am, that which I find myself a part of. I can hear her breathing now, rhythmically, slow, deep, and the howling sounds from outside juxtaposed against her soft breath.

"i can feel you staring at me"

"Oh I, I'm not-"

"go to sleep"

"I'm sorry."

"mhm"

I close my eyes but it makes no difference. The darkness looks the same. My brain feels the same too, my entire body feels the same. Almost like I exist all alone in this place, lying on the ground next to a harsh rocky formation, nature outside and nothing in except that soft breath. In out, in out, in out. I try to match it with my own breathing but my body calls for more air, I start taking deeper breaths, every exhale feels like a gust of wind against my own chest, a gust of wind against the tent, a gust of wind carrying me away into the darkness. I'm tired, so tired and alone. Please let me be. Please let me go. I just want to sleep.

Sleep.

March 11

Screaming. Shouting from somewhere. It is loud, what's loud? Someone's yelling, where? I am having trouble opening my eyes, sleep plagues them still and the light is too bright. Light? I hold my arm over my brow and peer ahead, the tent has been ripped away, remnants of the base remain, and there are people running about. Screaming. Shouting from everywhere.

"HEY! GRAB THE BAG," a figure calls out to me. Did I hear that right? Bag, what bag? I blink rapidly, clearing my eyes, the right is still stuck closed. I breathe in and the air gets stuck in my throat, coughing, hacking, nothing comes up yet I am still unable to breathe. Smoke. It's thickening the air, heavy, burning, my lungs hurt like a sore muscle. I am going to die. Suffocate and die. Where is the bag? I can feel my heart beat in my ears, revolving around my head, dizzy. I shuffle around everything lying on the ground, the hat Drew gave me for the trip is under the torn fabrics of the bed roll Cynthia had slept in. Is she okay? I look around for a moment and spot people fighting, she must be there if so, a warrior with her weaponry. I grab the hat, coughing again, much worse this time, I can't stop, my throat hurts, each cough reverberates in the back of my mouth. I am going to curl up next to the rocks and die.

"What the fuck are you doing?"

"The bag," I look up to see one of Maude's men, he is wearing a mask that covers only his nose and mouth. He grabs my face and brings it up to him, forcing a similar mask onto me.

"Make sure it's tight." He throws me over his shoulder and starts running. I secure the mask with one hand, gripping the hat in my other, the only thing I have left. I can breathe now but my throat is still tight. I try to speak but nothing more than a rasp comes out. Looking around I see we're leaving, the fighting growing quieter, the figures shrinking. Most of them lie in the dirt now, impossible to tell who or what, but I know for certain many have died in this moment. I could have died, maybe I should have, now I will starve in the woods above Maladi, a slow, painful death, lost, alone with this man I do not even know. At least we will die together. Now that we're far enough away, the sky above our campsite is visible, well, the sky isn't, but the black clouds are. The large, wispy masses of smoke that block out the sun, casting an elongated shadow across the trees. The rays coming through the leaves appear grey. Oh what a sight.

"Are you awake?"

"Yes," I eke out a sound.

"When we reach the platform you're going to be in charge of the lever, do you understand?"

"I wasn't taught how."

"It only moves forward and backward."

"Oh."

"Do you understand?"

"Where are you going?"

"To see if I can recover anyone else. Then regroup with the others."

"Who else survived?" He does not answer immediately, he's been running for minutes with me on his shoulder and he struggles to catch his breath.

"Here." All of a sudden I am launched from his shoulder, his hands on my hips I am swung backward onto the platform. With a loud thud I land next to a few crates on my left, and a group of unmoving bodies on my right. He jogs alongside the platform.

"The lever, keep the platform moving, I'll be back." Heel to the ground, he turned back and ran. In a few seconds he disappeared behind the slope of the hill. I put the hat on and sit up. My body hurts, not from the unceremonious slam, but from being tense for too long. My eyes are already heavy. This is too much for me. I want to go home. Thousands of miles away, I can feel the softness of my blankets, rubbing across my skin as I move around in my cool, dark room, reading a book with a lamp at my side. I do not think I will ever see that again. I can only go forward, down the hill, away from the enemy, into the unknown. I can only go forward. The platform gives a violent lurch and I slide into the crates. I manage to stand up only for it to stutter again, this time I fall over one of the shorter boxes and land on the edge of the wood. We are slowing down. The lever. I walk towards it and just as I am about to pull the rod into me, a hand from the mass of bodies grasps the pole and moves it forward.

"youre supposed to do that before the rail malfunctions"

"No one taught me."

"going to get us killed" I recognize that voice, sweet but snappy.

"You made it?"

"of course i did", she sits up, looking into my eyes and smiling. She holds her arm out for me to help her up, and I do. Before doing anything, else she reaches for one of the crates, prying it open and digging around inside. She produces two small pouches and tosses one to me. "you only get one a day so make it last"

"Thank you." She nods. She begins organizing the crates, taking things out of one and putting them into another. I sit on the back edge

16

of the platform, legs dangling over the side, almost low enough to touch the ground, grazing the grass as we move along. Inside the pouch there is not much, a whole day's worth? Clearly not. A few cubes of bread, a slice of dried meat, and a little glass bottle with a cork in it.

"What's in the bottle?" The glass is far too dark to see into, or the liquid is the same blue as the glass, and it does not smell like anything.

"dinner", she works almost frantically, her hands and arms moving quick and shaking, "will fill you up like an entire meal"

"I see." Three meals, breakfast, lunch, and dinner. How sad. I take out the bread cubes and bite into one of them. Surprisingly it's not dry, the texture of a muffin without the flavor. My stomach gurgles, moves inside my abdomen with a mind of its own, I am tempted to drink the liquid, maybe just a sip.

"you have to save it", she gives me a stern look. I nod.

"Do you think anyone else survived?"

"probably not"

"And that doesn't concern you at all?"

"did i kill them", I furrow my brow, "could i have saved them myself"

"No."

"right so what do you want me to do"

"I don't know."

"im going back to help casey after i eat"

"What about me?"

"what about you"

"I don't know anything about the platform or our supplies."

"what do you think ive been doing", she pulls me up and holds her arm out towards the crates, "i laid everything out and put likes together"

"I'm sorry."

"its not your fault im just unlucky to get you instead of a warrior", I nod. This is a tough place, I understand now, I do not belong. I always

17

thought I would be able to fight, be strong, but I am nothing. I want to be strong so badly. Why was I given a body so weak, so exhausted and downtrodden, only to live as if I am already dead. Why am I here?

"What happens if you don't come back?"

"you make it to the bottom hopefully"

"How long will that take?"

"three days maybe four with imperfect lever timing"

"And there's enough food for all of us?"

"those are dead bodies", I look over at the few that lay at the back of the platform, how clueless can I be? They have not moved an inch since I arrived. "theyll bury them in maladi once you get there"

"Okay." Cynthia grabs my arm just under the band and looks at me, for a moment I feel she is scared too, what I thought was frantic shaking is trembling, fear. She does not linger here. In one motion she retrieves a long blade from her leg and flips it toward me.

"if anyone without a band moves near the platform you have to kill them"

"Okay."

"ill be back with casey by the end of the day", she grabs a bag which she had filled with a few of the pouches and various other supplies, "i promise"

"Be careful. Please."

"always", with that she jumps off the platform and begins running up the slope in the same direction Casey had gone. The smoke had cleared a bit as it congregated in one area and drifted up into the infinite sky. Light now poured onto me, the trees were thinning and when I look ahead I can see large open fields of grass and what looks like wheat or corn. Wild growths. Surely there are no farmers here, though of course I do not know. There are people who live in the woods, the ones who attacked us, and I presume Cynthia and the others came from this area too. If she left me alone it must be safer the further down we get. I push the lever and sit down on the front ledge to keep watch. The platform speeds up over a few seconds and begins shaking side to side. I can feel the wind on my face, hear the sound of the platform grazing the grass. Push the lever too early and it moves too fast, too late and we all go flying off as it comes to a halt. It will slow down eventually. I just need to wait.

I wake up and the sun is already halfway down, we are hardly moving and my feet are dragging along the ground. The slope had smoothed out while I was asleep and flat plains extend in all directions as far as the eye can see. I do not remember lying down. Lucky we did not get attacked. We. I, really. I find it much easier to say we, easier to cope with the presence of sunbathing corpses, and easier to avoid acknowledging my ostracization as of late. No one has returned to the platform that I know of, everything is exactly how it was before. The sun. They will not make it here without the light of day. Can you even start a fire on this? I'm unsure whether that's a good idea anyway. The light may attract more attention than the loud clunks of the rail. It was windy last night and we were among the trees, so I can only imagine the great gusts that are sure to rend my body. Cold, dark, sad, and lonely. If only I could reach out and slow the sun's descent myself, hold it in my hand and breath in the fiery warmth it radiates. I can only wish.

I lift myself up and retrieve my food pouch. I guess I missed lunch. Biting into the dried meat I walk to the lever and push it down slowly, the platform accelerates and I pull it back before we get too fast. The mask still hangs around my neck but I think I'll be okay without it. I take it off along with my hat and shirt, setting them in one of the empty crates I assume is for storage. There must be water to bathe with somewhere in here. I look through two of the boxes before I am able to find it, a large glass jar full of water, there are three of them. As not to waste the water I'll also need to drink, I only pour a little into my hand rubbing it on my face, down my neck and over my chest and shoulders.

The water drips down my body, hanging onto every hair, working its way down my face, almost feels as if I could wash away this reality. I could throw water in my eyes, opening them to reveal a nice sunset back home, walking along the sidewalk groceries in hand, if only. I can never wash off Maladi. It's in me, writhing and squirming in every part of my body, creeping along every inch of my muscle and skin, slithering out my throat from within, filling my chest so I cannot breathe. I feel it will last forever. Even if I manage to make it back home, would I belong there anymore? Would anyone be able to recognize who I am now? I am unchanged, yet in every way I resemble something new, as if each part of my body and soul were switched with identical parts of similar function. I feel strange.

I pull my shirt back on and place the hat back atop my head. I return to the front edge and sit, opening the cork to the little blue bottle. I smell it again even though I know there will be no odor, swirl it around a few times, and down the entire liquid in one swig. It tastes like nothing, but the texture is different than anything I have ever drank. Thick, almost solid like slime, chalky and abrasive on the way down, the entire surface of my mouth coated in a layer of film that will not come off no matter what I do. I feel full, however. Cynthia was right, this could last me the entire day if I did not do much, which I didn't. I may have made the mistake of sleeping on watch, but it saved me the pain of waiting in silence for hours through hunger and thirst and the worst kind of boredom, the kind where you feel like screaming because you spent so much time whispering to yourself, like you must yell or you will explode. Cynthia. I am becoming skeptical that either of them will return. There could be others, four platforms in total. Am I the first of the four? I cannot remember, I wasn't paying attention on the back of Casey, what did we pass? It's possible then they made it to a different one, or passed me altogether. Drew could be alive somewhere. We'll have to reconvene in Maladi. All paths lead down.

The sun is passing below the crops standing watch on the horizon. I guess I should sleep once again, I need to be awake at first light. This time I'll sleep with the blade she gifted me and tomorrow's food pouch. I push the lever forward a bit and gather my things, accidentally kicking one of the bodies. I neglected to look at them the entire day, I'm afraid I may see someone I know, afraid I may see Drew, nor do I want to see the lifeless bodies that I lay next to in my sleep. But, now I am curious with the last light fading, casting shadows across their hiding faces. I place my foot on the shoulder of the closest, rotating the limp mass toward me, the head rolls and smacks into the platform, falling too low to see the features.

I get on my knees, one arm holding me up I use the other to guide the face to mine. I stare into the empty eyes, they are wide open, still in shock, frozen in time. The cheek still soft to the touch, I caress it gently. I can almost feel the air coming out of their nose, small, soft breaths. I press my forehead onto their's, feeling the soul still trapped in their body, the warmth collecting and transferring into my skin. Many minutes pass like this. My eyes closed at some point and when I opened them the sun was below the horizon, all light gone; but, I can still see into their eyes. The white stands out so vibrant, the part with no life, the part that does not see. They look like my eyes the longer I stare, so much so that I would believe they were mine if I could not feel them in my skull. Are they in my skull? I lay the head down and get up to just one knee. Slowly, I reach towards my face, fingers grabbing at my right eye, I rub the surface and feel its moistness. It has a thin, slimy layer that does not come off with my touch. I give a slight press and there is some resistance similar to rubber, but feels soft and buoyant like jam. I shake my hand off and stand up. The moon is rising now and provides little light, though it is enough for me to make my way to the lever. Again I press it forward. We must go faster.

I lay down at the front of the platform. I refrain from swinging my legs over the edge as I may awake to rough greenery, there is no way to know what comes next. Staring up at the sky I see the stars. There are many, some bright and some so distant they are not more than a speck of dust that shone white on the black surface. I set my things next to me and raise my arms into the air. My fingers look so short, my hands small and stocky, why can I not have nice, elegant, smooth hands? I should remove them for they betray me. Every last one. No. I am tired. I should sleep. Sleep and begin anew tomorrow. I lay one arm across my face to shield my eyes from the white light being cast down from the sky. My other rests on my heart. The beat is strong unlike the rest of my body. Each one pounds like a war drum, rumbling my organs, rippling into my hand. Soon it is the only thing I can feel. One two. One two. One, Two Two, One. I wish I was strong. One Two. I wish I could have saved Drew. One, Two. Why me? One Two. Why must I suffer in this frail body. One Two Three, One. I wish I was powerful.

I open my eyes to see nothing. I must have been asleep, though it feels like no time passed at all. I did not dream, I did not move, I felt nothing. Where is the moon? The stars? There is no light at all. Less than when the sun first set. I sit up. I can still feel the platform moving, hear its hum as it slides along the rails, but I cannot see the surface I sit on. I raise my hand to my face but it is not there. Nothing is there. The sound of beasts calling out to one another, a deep gurgling howl, shoots out far to my right. My head turns quickly. The air is turning cold, feels as if someone is breathing it onto me. I reach for the crates to find something to cover with to no avail. Where are the crates? The howls get louder, closer. I hear the gnashing of teeth. I can barely move my hands, frozen, shaking uncontrollably. No. I shake my head in a violent motion. I close my eyes. No. It can't be. The platform slams into the ground, one of the beasts landed atop, its claws scraping along the wood. Howling once more, he tears into the platform with what I can only imagine are jaws of unwieldy proportions. I am hanging on with the tips of my fingers, so cold the bones feel like they will snap. I shake my head, even more vicious than before, brain rattling in its case. No! I hear the beast prepare for a lunge, but before it is able to I close my eyes with such force they might pop and I scream. I scream for what feels like an eternity. When I stop, the beast finally propels itself at me, as I feel the tips of its teeth touch my skin I scream

into

darkness.

March 12

I breathe in and look around the room. My fist rests on my cheek, I am bored. Endless talking and complaints and bills and so called justice! Ha! Alas, I wish they would just take care of everything for me, it is not like I do much.

"I do not think it is worth the trouble." My commander, and most trusted knight, speaks on my right. His voice booms over the hall and it brings my attention back..

"Please sir. They took my brother. And half the men we had watching over the farmland. Please." The young boy's voice quivering, he sits on his knees, begging for our help. The lower hills farmland. They reached this far into our territory, bold, but why?.

"Maude, it is our most valuable holding," I interject, turning my head to the commander.

"Indeed. Almost all of last year's grain came from the lower hills," she did not speak often, but when she did it was always to comment on the managerial, technical aspect of our kingdom. We must do something if not to show our force, the yield is already going to be low despite any setbacks.

"One raid is nothing to worry about," a staunch reply from Maude.

"How can you say that when they hold our families hostage!" The young boy stands and rushes up a few steps before he is knocked down by one of the royal guards.

"And you expect us to ride out to save them? PAH! We'd be fools to engage the Uttarack in open combat," Maude moves to set the proposal aside, but I grab his wrist before he can. I read over the paper: a raid in the early hours of the morning just as the sun was rising, goblins everywhere, many people lost or taken, many badly injured, crops and store houses razed. It is dangerous, yes, but we may be able to recover the hostages.

"How do you know the ones taken are still alive?" I call down to the boy still laying on his back, the wind knocked out of him. He holds back the tears I see in his eyes, how sad.

"They threw them in wagons," weak and defeated he is.

"The men surely would have been slaughtered in the field if they wanted to kill them," my fair Princess Lila, sitting a few steps down, offers her advice. Her voice so smooth and light, the words hit my skin like the rays of sunshine on a spring morning. She takes pity on the boy it seems.

"So they want us to ride out," again with the technical, Cynthia the spymaster, I knew she would be the voice of reason. I fall too often into the trust of my love. I must not pity the boy lest I leave our people exposed. The farmland.

"And if we ride out we will definitely perish," Maude puts his hand on my shoulder, "Sire, it's not smart."

"Can we send a small party, a squad of five or so? Then the castle remains guarded and we may have a chance to bargain." A compromise is usually the best, though Maude will know it is not a true compromise. If our men get into danger, they will simply ride away. He smiles.

"Let it be so, but I will not be riding with them," he is too stubborn - a good quality for a leader, but he lacks the loyalty one would expect as his ruler.

"Nestor," I call for my squire standing in the farthest corner of the

25

hall, "prepare my armor and the Sword of The Pheonix. We leave at first light."

"Yes sire," he pushes his way out of the crowded doorway, disappearing around the corner. I need more courtiers like him.

"You can't. I will not allow it," Princess Lila stands now, back to the hall, looking directly into my eyes. Just as I am about to respond, Cynthia speaks:

"Sending yourself is more foolish than riding the entire garrison, you'll either die or start an all out war."

"The lion which cares for the cub remains in the pride past his time," the old chaplain loves his sayings.

"I must go myself. I would not command anyone to their death. Nor would I risk losing our best soldiers."

"So you will die yourself?" Princess Lila rises up to my throne, cupping my left cheek with her soft, cold hand.

"Of course not. Maude, round up the coursers, and give me four of your best riders," before he can react I grab his shirt and pull him down to me, moving away from the princess' grasp, speaking under my breath, "riders, do you understand?"

"At once sire," he nods and heads down the stairs, taking one moment to look at the boy still sitting on the floor, then striding out the same tall oak doors Nestor departed through.

"Then it is decided!" I decree into the hall, loud enough so the common folk outside the doors can hear, "I will ride against the Uttarack at dawn, and we will return with the lives of our brothers and sisters!"

"May the scorn of the gods reach into their souls, wresting what little life they have from their bosom, and disposing it in our treasury." It is good to know someone believes in me.

"Thank you, sir. Thank you so much," the little boy is back on his knees, looking up the steps.

26

"It is not for you, it is for all mankind."

"Of course sir."

"Cynthia, push the rest of the proposals to next week. Everyone is dismissed."

"May I send a few scouts to the lower hills?" Oh Cynthia.

"Do as you wish, whatever you think may aid my adventure."

"At once," Cynthia gathers her books and goes out the door on our right, the old chaplain follows her, hobbling along as fast as he can. The rest of the citizens and guards exit as well, courtiers shuffle around the hall as they clean up, arranging the hall for the provisional council which will sit while I am away. Hollow wood sounds echo off the stone walls, the occasional clang of metal reaches my throne, I can almost hear the people speaking of my bravery from the streets of the castle.

"Lila."

"Yes my love," she did not even look at me, simply continuing to organize her table. I do not say anything else. I rise from my seat and walk out the side door. As soon as the door closes behind me, the wet air hits my face. I take a deep breath - how refreshing. The clouds block the sun and the sky altogether, but I can see the light illuminating my people, the gods casting their favor upon me. I lean on the wooden railing and look down on the streets. People everywhere, children running, playing in the mud, dogs barking, the market square bustling, I must return for these people. From my vantage point - the keep sits at the very top of the centermost hill with the city unfolding below - I can even see outside the walls. Somewhere in the woods the Uttarack stow away with my subjects. Oh how they will pay.

I push myself off the railing and continue down the path to my quarters. The door is already open when I arrive. I hear the clinking of soft metal as I approach. Swinging the door aside I see Nestor handling my armor, he's brought three different pairs. As soon as he notices my presence he stands up straight, waiting for my command.

"It's okay Nestor."

"I thought you might want to choose, Sire."

"I do." I examine the sets, my usual is set up on the armor stand, and the other two laid across my grand table. I like the color and comfort of my normal armor, but I think it will be far too easy to slice through, too many gaps and the metal is soft on the inside. I take one look at the armors on the table and turn to Nestor, "Can you procure something heavier? I want chain under thick steel plates."

"Don't you think it might be too difficult to run in if necessary?"

"I do. But run I will not."

"Maude has told the men that is the plan."

"Plans change. You're coming with us so get yourself some armor too." I reach into the chest at the foot of my bed, grabbing a little pouch and tossing it to him.

"Yes sire. I shall leave yours in my quarters until the morning."

"That will do."

He nods and leaves the room in a hurry, slamming the door behind him. The chest still open, I reach in again and find my crown. I run my fingers over the gems encrusted into the sides, it still glistens in the light even after all these years. I close the chest and set the crown on the table next to my armors. I will not be wearing these sets but I will no doubt ride against the Uttarack with my crown sitting high. A knock comes at my door.

"Come in." It is the Princess Lila, I can tell from the way she knocks, so gentle yet firm in rhythm. She slips between the crack in the door and shuts it behind her. Waltzing to me almost as if she floats just above the ground, she grabs my face again, both hands on my cheeks, and kisses me. Every time I feel her touch, despite her cold skin, the warmth of a fire rushes through our connection, straight into my heart, turning my stomach. She looks me in the eyes and sighs, a soft, telling sigh.

"I am going to be okay," I grab her hands and guide them down, moving along her arms until I get to her shoulders, pulling her in, wrapping her delicate body in my arms. "I promise Li."

"Your promise means nothing when you aren't in charge of keeping it. What will you do if they take you too? Thrash your body until I can't even recognize your beautiful face? What will I do?"

"I'll do what I always do," I let her go and guide her to the bed, picking her up by the waist and throwing her down onto the mass of quilts and furs, "I'll find my way back to you even if it means taking the world down in flames." She laughs as I slip out of my outer wear, laying down next to her.

"Seriously! I will worry until you say you will not go."

"Then you are doomed to worry until I return."

"Promise me you will ride away at the first sign of danger."

I turn on my side, placing my hand on her neck, fingers in the back of her hair, "I promise."

Her eyes reveal her mistrust, they are hard, like those of an owl, "What's gotten into you?"

"Nothing I can't handle," I smile, her face softens a little.

"This isn't like you."

"It is, I just normally don't know how to show it."

"And maybe that's a good thing."

"Maybe it was." We look into each other's eyes for a while, our breaths alternating, hers too short to stay in rhythm with mine. It begins raining again, thunder rumbling across the hills, the patter of the drops against the window panes. "But I am going to be strong now. For me, and you, and everyone."

She does not say anything, rather she closes her eyes and lays a fur over herself. I take my hand off her and move her hair out of the way, kissing her on the forehead. I slide off the bed and pull the curtains closed to deafen the storm sounds, then snuff out all the lights but one, the one in my small hand lantern. I pick up the clothes I slipped off and throw them into a bin, here I take off the rest of my clothes, exposing my bare skin to the slightly moist air, even in this room in the inner corridors you can never escape the aura outside. I enter the second, smaller room where I store my things and maintain a large barrel of fresh water. I dip my hands in it, feeling the cool liquid envelope them. I trace my fingers along the lines of my palm ,causing ripples to form in the small pool. I cup my hands and splash water onto my face, rubbing my eyes, letting the water fall down my cheeks and onto my neck. A deep breath. I bend over and peer into the barrel. It's me, but not at the same time. There's something different about my reflection, maybe it's the flame from the lantern which flickers, casting my face in waves across the water, or maybe I am just tired.

Lightning strikes out the window in front of me, straight down to the ground, far out into the woods. It cracks so loud I jump, shaking the barrel. In the moment of blue light I see something new in the water, just for a moment I can see my features, sharp like never before, yet there is a slice reaching from just above my right brow down to the left side of my neck, blood dripping everywhere. What? The ensuing thunder caused the flame from the lantern to burn out. Quickly I reset it, holding the lantern to the water this time, so close the water threatens to eat it alive; but, I see nothing. Just the soft outline of my face. With my free hand I scoop a bit more water and toss it over my eyes, rubbing them once more. I blink a few times and move back into the main room. Lila had turned on her side, now curled into a ball under multiple quilts and furs. I set the lantern down on the bedside table, snuff the flame, and lay next to her. I must sleep to gather my energy. I must sleep to be strong. And when I awake I will be the lion I was always meant to be. I must. I turn on my side as well, pressing my body into hers, wrapping her close to me, and I close my eyes.

March 13

We ride in a loose formation. A gang of six bandits atop horses with strong legs and slim builds, riding the main road in search of weak travelers with treasure galore. Except we adorn the sigil of my oldest ancestor upon our breast, and beneath it the finest metalwork on this side of the ridge, and at my hip the sword forged in magma from the center of the Earth bearing a gemstone carved of the same insignia - the Sword of the Phoenix. We are no bandits. We are the men who will send the Uttarack crawling back into their burrows. We are the royal envoy, led by the ruler of our kingdom. Yet, we ride relaxed. Talking like friends, joking like family, no eyes on the road. Our only thoughts are on the feast that awaits our return, the barrels and barrels of wine we shall acquire from the boys of the farmland. And mine of returning to the fair Princess Lila, to feel her smooth skin against mine, her soft breaths touching my cheek. I will return as a hero. The Hero of Amiens, Warrior of the Phoenix, Liberator of People, me with my five men, my trusty squad, we will prevail.

"Do we know where they're stationed?" The conversation turns to tactics now that we approach the expansive fields, full of tall crops for leagues.

"Not exactly. One of the scouts said she saw an Uttarack woman down by the brook gathering buckets of water, so their camp must be near there," I guess her tactics had proved useful.

"You know the brook runs across our entire countryside," the bowman with the long, thick brown hair seems rather concerned, a man who has seen many battles.

"Yes yes, where was it again Nestor?"

"At Pilter's Rock, sir."

"Underground," the mace wielder catches on a bit slowly, let's hope strong.

"Precisely. I would be lying if I said I wasn't a bit concerned myself," I would be lying either way.

"We'll have to bargain outside."

"That's if they even come out to greet us."

"Ha! Good luck getting an Uttarack to leave the burrow."

"I'm surprised you left yours."

"I say we send you in first, ask for their good grace."

"Me!?"

"If they come out it'll be in full force."

"You're the quickest, have the best chance of making it up the rocks on foot."

"Who said I'd be on foot?"

"We might be able to take their fighters if we use the water to our advantage."

"How's that? We have no equipment."

"Well you damn well can't ride a horse into a cavern."

"We fight in the water, the armors should hold us down even if the current's strong."

"Which we hope it will be."

"Right."

"Have you ever tried?"

"Of course not! Your horse would slip and you'd break both your necks."

33

"Maybe my horse is special."

"Makes two of you."

The conversation derails and everyone is back in a jolly mood. Laughing and singing, Maude gave me the right people. The man with the golden helm rides up next to me, we are at the front of the pack now, riding in pairs of two. He speaks without looking at me, his eyes penetrating the tree line:

"We should make a fighting plan, delegate positions."

"I agree. You know your brothers better than I."

"Aye. Normally I lead with the mace wielder at my side. You'll be the right flank, Nestor on the left, and the last swordsman by the bowman in the rear. Is that alright?"

"Sounds perfect. About the strategy with the water," he interrupts me, though I may have paused for too long between words allowing this misstep.

"I think it's a good one. Uttarack wear light armor. We just need to lure them out and station in the brook."

"Won't our movement be severely inhibited?"

"Undoubtedly. But in this position they should be forced to bargain or face a fight on our own terms."

"So fleeing is off the table?" I would not have called for a rout anyway, but if the plan to fight was the helmsman's idea... This may prove to be entertaining. We are passing under the first trees, the warm sunlight leaving our presence. I find myself on edge. We are in their territory now, even though this land belongs to me! The air smells of wet wood, surely the sun could not reach beneath the leaves and dry last evening's rain, but the smell is so strong.

"I don't foresee any of us making it past this tree line even with a head start," he speaks very seriously, calm even despite our impending - some might call hopeless - battle. Clearly an experienced warrior like the bowman, though he has an extra sense, a leader for many years perhaps, I can see the experience of near death in the corners of his eyes. I trust him.

"Neither did I."

"We should refrain from telling the others. Call upon us when the moment arises, and we will give our all."

"Yes Captain," I smile and he turns to look at my face for the first time since we began speaking. The corner of his mouth moves slightly, right eye winking. He pulls his reins, slowing the horse to a trot, and turns back toward the others. The formation breaks back into the puddle-like grouping we had been in before. I push my horse forward. I think it's time we see Pilter's Rock, if we're quick we should arrive within the hour. Even though I am ready for a fight, the fight of my life, bargaining comes first. What strategy should I take? Force? Trade? Or might we arrange some sort of treatise, I could allow them to stay in the cavern as long as they do not enter the lower hills or harass my citizens. I guess I'll need to know what they want. Too bad Cynthia's spies couldn't learn that for me, that's their main disadvantage - they are still human. No human faces the Uttarack, yet I ride on. And so do the five others, each as brave as I. But not I. The Captain, the mace wielder, the bowman, the swordsman, and Nestor of course. Each with their own life they put on the line today, to die is to lose everything, to die is to lose I, yet we ride on. We act as one from now on, I must be them, I must not die, I as in we, and we as in us. Where is the light in this place, oh gods? I look to the sky and see nothing but leaves and thick branches and horrid hanging vines. Where is the light to guide me? Where are you when I need you most, which is always, but especially now? No matter how long I wait, you never come, every day tomorrow, every day I wait, and tomorrow is when, not tomorrow if today is tomorrow but tomorrow as the next day from today, which is every day. Oh gods, why!

"Sir," I almost fall off my horse from the scare Nestor gave me, riding up next to me so quickly, "I'm sorry, didn't mean to interrupt your thought. But, the rock."

He points ahead and I see the huge mound of smooth stone arching over a downhill slope, the entrance to the cavern. On the right is the brook the Captain spoke of earlier, it is rushing today from the strong storm and there is just enough clearing between the rock and the shoreline to create a funnel as the greenery is too thick to traverse elsewhere. Everything is going according to plan. It's perfect. We just need to lure them out. Oh gods, give us your grace so that we may slay the Uttarack at the top of this slope, among this thick, evil wood. We reach the clearing. A mere field length away from the entrance we sit atop our horses, waiting.

"I still think he should go first."

"I think we should take a vote."

"I vote you."

"I vote you too."

"This is beyond unfair."

"Everyone stop. First things first, we need to swim our horses across, then we'll decide. Rationally."

"Yes Captain," they all say in unison. He is to be our leader from now until the end it seems. He goes first, slowly treading the horse into the waves at the shore, and I follow. My horse is apprehensive at first, rearing a bit as his first hoof touched the water, it must be cold. We will have to stand in it for as long as the negotiations take and fight in it if we are so lucky, a perfect but precarious plan. The water is not too deep but the current is strong, it pushes the horse slowly downstream as it reaches their underbelly. Almost certainly the water will crawl up to the bottom of my chest at the middle most section. A smart but dangerous plan. We reach the other side and tie the horses to the trees closest to the shore. However, they are still a good distance away. It would surely be an all out sprint if we needed to reach them. Plus they are on the wrong side of the brook - it might take an entire day to ride down to the bridge in the far east as there is no possibility of ferrying the horses back across with Uttarack archers at our back. I am thinking too much. We have not even made first contact.

"I'll volunteer to call upon them," I say, and everyone stops what they are doing to look at me.

"I was thinking either myself or the Captain would do it since we're at the front of the formation."

"It should be the mace wielder, he's the most intimidating," the bowman slings his quiver on and straps his bag to his horse.

"I agree," Nestor speaking on battle plans, a sight I thought I would never see. Actually, one I had never thought of to begin with.

"Aye," the Captain has decided, whether through the sentiments of the crew or through a choice he had already made, it did not matter. We are to follow his orders.

"Alright. Let's go then," we must not wait any longer, perhaps we did not wait long enough, but who is to decide when the time is right? So I command the commencement of our plan.

"Nestor," we walk alongside each other with heavy feet, our metal crushing the sticks, crunching on the leaves under us, "I'm sorry for bringing you here."

"Sir. It would be an honor to die by your side. May they tear me limb from limb before I fall in your defense."

"May the gods grant us your wish," we wade into the water, up to my thighs now it rushes between the metal strapped to my body. I feel its cool presence caressing my skin, soaking every fiber of the wool clothes I wear, soaking every pore and hair of mine. Each step is more like a shuffle, forcing my legs forward from the hip, constantly locking my knees to counteract the pressure that wants to take me to the left, downstream. The water is loud too, I had not realized until now. All the sounds of the birds and wind on the leaves and rabbits dashing after each other and metal clinking together, all gone, replaced by my thoughts and the unbearable sound of rushing water. It overwhelms my ears, coming from every direction, right left up down inside, almost as if the water flows through my own ears, swirling in my skull, pressing its way out through any hole it can find. My head feels like it will explode. The pressure is too great. I look down and my hand is in a fist, bright red, wrapped around the hilt of my sword. I'm ready. I always have been.

I assume my position on the right. Nestor looks at me and nods, holding his hand to his heart, and begins the slow trudge to the left side of the group. We stand just before the halfway point of the crossing so the brook is shallow enough to stand, but deep enough to cause havoc. I turn and see the bowman further back standing on the downward slope into the water, the swordsman just below him. I turn back and I wince, the sun caught my right eye as it bounces off the helm of the Captain, the sun which is directly above us now, yet hardly visible but through reflections. I look down and see the light, rushing like the water, bouncing with each ripple and wave. I hold my hand out, palm up, over the spot where the single ray of light shone down. The colored iron of my gauntlet gathers little of that light, but it is enough for me to see the minuscule divots, thin scratches, blemishes in the forgery, this man made armor. Something man has made which I trust against those which came from nothing. My armor cannot stand forever, but it must stand for today. I reach up to the light which comes through a small part in the leaves hanging on branches larger than a small home. Oh gods, please grant us your light, may you shine on us today and give my blade a fire it has never felt before!

I look to where the Captain and the mace wielder had been standing, but neither was there. At the mouth of the cavern, under the great arch of Pilter's Rock, is the Captain. He peers over what appears to me to be an edge, as if one must enter the cavern by leaping off a cliff, though I know that is not so. The elevation plays tricks on my eyes; and water on my ears, light on my mind. I will not be fooled any longer. When the Uttarack arise with the mace wielder at the front of their entourage, I will face them, I will stand here among my brothers, in the presence of the gods, and I will take back what is ours. I will no longer sit back and watch as others do, I must not. Perhaps I waited too long for this day, perhaps I never thought it would never come, perhaps it was I holding me back, believing there was no hope. But, there must be, right? What is life without hope, what am I without dreams? I am nothing. But, today I am something. I am.

"He's coming back! Everyone at the ready," the Captain calls back to us as he draws his weapon, slowly stepping back from the cavern. My body tenses, hand back on the hilt of my blade. Out of the corner of my eye I see Nestor with his sword halfway out of the sheath, shaking incredibly much, only then I realize I am too. No matter how hard I focus, both my hands shake, my strength depleted, I feel hot. In my head and crawling down my skin, I feel a warmth like a fever except it boils hotter, overflowing into my eyes. There's pressure in my head too, the stress has been building up for too long. I need to breathe.

The mace wielder appears but he is not running like I had imagined. He walks a few paces ahead of an Uttarack who is himself a few paces ahead of a group of three more. None of them are the leader, I can tell, they wear basic leather fittings and carry basic weapons, two with axes and two with swords. I remember back when I took lessons from the old chaplain, the Uttarack nobility never wore armor nor carried any weapon besides their long claws, and they most definitely would not come out to greet what appears to be a group of vagabonds. Maybe this will be easier than I thought. Not only are they common goblins, but there's only four of them.

The Captain and mace wielder walk together to the brook, conversing about something. I wonder what he saw in the cavern, I wish I could have seen for myself, soon I may very well. The goblin group had stopped at the halfway point between the cavern and the shore, just far enough that we would have to shout to communicate and neither side could reasonably reach the other without warning. They are cautious, I can use that to my advantage. To prey on the threat of danger without being outright threatening.

"You there! What's your name?" I call out to none of them in particular, I wish to discern who will take charge. The Captain and mace wielder take their positions in the water below the shoreline. I'm nervous, but we have the planning advantage on our side. Instead of responding, the goblins turn to each other and laugh - a gross and liquidy sound - speaking in their own language. The old chaplain had gone over basic phrases with me but I remember none of it now, not that I paid enough attention back then anyways.

"What's so funny?" The Captain yells at them, his voice rough and menacing, to me at least.

"What fool wears a full set of armor, but leaves a crown atop his head!" They burst out into laughter again, even louder than before.

"A prince of course," I speak loud enough for them to hear, but I will yell no longer, if they wish they can step forward. We need to establish a strong arm if we want to get our people back.

"And what *prince* would that be?"

"I'm the Prince of Amiens, the kingdom you fiends raided just yesterday; and I've come for my people. Hand them over and we'll leave promptly."

"The Prince of Amiens…" One of the goblins spoke under his breath and leapt back into the cavern. May I have revealed too much? No. Surely he goes to retrieve his leader, then the real negotiations can begin.

"I command you to bring your leader to our presence, we're here to negotiate."

"Yes yes, your friend already told us. Why do you think *we're* here!"

"They mock you, sir," Nestor speaks to me without taking his eyes off the measly goblins, anger in his brow.

"I know. Let them dwell in their arrogance, we will have our time."

"Of course sir."

"How many hostages are in your camp?" I command them to tell me, they need to know I am unaffected by their trickery.

"However many it takes to feed three hundred Uttarack!" These three must find everything hilarious as they begin laughing again.

"You ate the hostages?" The mace wielder questions.

"You saw them with your own eyes didn't you? I would never eat a human, they taste of rotten elf-loins."

"Good to know," a snarl on his face, the Captain is growing more agitated by the second, that must be what they want, to prod us into going over the edge. If we leave the water that would be the end of us, or if they engage in a full ambush, we must not let negotiations go south. We need to remain calm and simply wait for their leader, clearly nothing productive is going to come from speaking with the commoners.

"I say we kill these three," the bowman had not said much the entire trip, but now he speaks in violence, "show them what happens when you cross us."

"If their leader does not come," I turn my head and nod to him, his hand wrapped around an arrow already, he lowers it and keeps the bow at his side. I face the goblins once more, but they are not there, where? Where did they go? "Was no one watching them?"

"I thought you were."

41

"I looked away for one second."

"I heard something on our left."

"There's only water on the left you idiot!"

"You didn't see them either."

"It wasn't my job."

"The whole expedition is our job."

"Hey!"

"We need to get out of here."

"Stay in the water!"

"Scan the trees."

"Sir!"

"I hear them coming out of the cavern."

"Draw your weapons."

"NOT YET!" I command. We will lose against their entire force.

"Guys!"

"WHAT?"

"Look around," I shift around in the water, moving carefully not to lift my feet too far from the river bed, the current is picking up. Our horses had been untied and loosed upon the woods, our supplies sent with them, goblins stand in their place, inching up to the shoreline. Goblins everywhere, crawling through the greenery, out of the bushes, in the trees above, hundreds hanging on the branches, swinging back and forth. They pour out of the cavern mouth by the hundreds as well, flooding the space that was once between us. Some even stand atop Pilter's Rock, armed with crossbows and various flaming objects - all of them are armed and dressed in the same leather armor the original three wore.

"Damned to hell," I fix the crown on my head, sliding it back upright, and take a deep breath. This is it.

"And now the negotiations begin," a voice from above, smooth and spoken like they had been practicing for hours. I look up and again the crown slips. Catching it with my right hand, left on the hilt of my sword, I see a horrendous beast fall from the largest branch of them all. When he hits the ground it rumbles, sending the water splashing over my chest, drops hitting my face. Its feet are covered in fur like the mane of a lion and equipped with rough, thick, pointed claws. The rest of its body has shorter hair, except the face where a beard larger than my entire person hangs just below a moist, bulging nose. It smiles with jagged yellow teeth like daggers.

"We should've known," the Captain hisses at us. He is right. How could we come all this way, yet neglect the thought of a higher power. The Uttarack could never have pulled off a raid, much less an encampment, on their own. And now we stand face to face with a real bugbear.

"We're in the wrong formation now," the bowman is afraid, before he was stationed the furthest back, but now he cowers only a mere stride or two from the repulsive face of the beast.

"Stand your ground, we have nothing to fear as of yet," I take a few steps and stand up straight, dropping my shoulders and raising my chin. I try to mask the waver in my voice by speaking rapidly and slightly deeper than usual, "I am the prince as I'm sure you've heard."

"Of course," that smile, the way he talks is sickening, I wish only to carve my own ears out. Both my hands curl into tight fists, my palms sting from my nails or the gauntlet metal cutting into them. "And I, am Zegruth. But, you may know me as the Fist of the South."

"Indeed not," I will not appease this beast. The smile leaves its face, a low growl erupting from his broad, firm chest.

"To come to our land and expect royal treatment is foolish."

"I expect no such thing."

"You speak like you do."

"I come as your guest Zegruth. We simply were not aware of your presence prior to this moment."

"Then why do you stand in the water?"

"As a safety precaution. I will not lie."

"You know now it will not save you. The stream will but tickle my knees," the smile returns, its tongue - a bumpy and slimy abomination - protruding from the bottom row of teeth.

"Aye," I borrow the Captain's favorite saying.

"So come out of the water, then we may talk like guests."

"I think we are just fine where we are."

"As you wish," with a quick hand gesture the goblins close in on us. To our backs they swarm the shore, almost touching the rushing water, to the sides they begin forming the curves of a circle, the ones previously in the trees scurry down the trunks, leaping onto the backs of the larger hobgoblins which carry three at a time. "Now explain to us why we should release the humans to you?"

"What is it that you want Zegruth?" I cannot keep my body still, my head shakes on its pedestal, my neck feels weak, everything does. My stomach twitches, my breaths uneven, lurching on every breathturn, eyes weightless as if they have left my skull, floating in a dizzying bout.

"It's not obvious? We come to take your kingdom," the goblins break out into an uproar that floods my ears. I wince and cover my right ear, the left hand still attached to my sword, but there is no escape. They are everywhere. The sound like water bubbling in the back of the throat, it's disgusting! Such foul animals. AH. I HATE THEM. I HATE IT. AH. I slam my hand into my ear, again and again, but nothing drowns them out. Blood slides down my face from the temple, creating a red pool in my hand, staining the bronzed metal. I raise that hand to the beast:

"That I cannot give you! And if I am to die the entirety of the woodland would be razed before facing your repulsive existence!"

"Thanks for the advice, *prince.*"

"I would sooner slice my own throat than go into your custody."

"Go ahead"

"I think you're mistaken. Even in death I, the Prince of Amiens, would never give up," Zegruth's nostrils flare, the wet, protruding nose jumps. He observes the goblins, scanning their masses, many of them unable to hold back, itching to tear flesh from bone. The wind is picking up, blowing drops of water onto my cheek, threatening to take the crown, my crown, off my head, A cloud blocks the gap in the leaves which the sun previously shone through. Dark, windy, wet, tense.

"Give me your best offer," just then a deep roar shot out of the cavern, shaking my chest, ringing through the metal of my armor. The sound of metal scraping on stone followed, heavy metal, clinking like shackles. Chains. It must be chains. Chains. No. It can't be. I shake my head. NO. Why now? Why here? Another roar. This time the goblins shake, getting down on their knees, shielding their heads. I look to Zegruth and he remains standing, smiling. Damn you beast! Remove thy smile. Stones fall from the top of Pilter's Rock, crashing and cracking on the ground below. The Captain and the mace wielder face the cavern. I cannot turn my back on Zegruth. But they're everywhere. Up down left right far close, in me now. I let them get inside. In my head. Get out of my head! Again they roar, three loud outbursts. Three.

"Fuck," I turn at the sound of Nestor's voice. Three hairless ogres stomp out of the cavern, dragging massive chains behind them which wrap around their necks. Skin hangs in flaps over their fat bodies. They have dark holes for ears and long arms with three fingers at the end of each. Globs of saliva flow over their lips, greasing the chains and their stomach flaps. Oh gods, please. Take me away from here. They stand taller than the outer walls of my castle. They trample the bushes and vines with ease, crushing them with heavy steps. Closer and closer. The thought of being crushed alive, bones crunching inside my skin, shattered and piercing my body. It can't be.

"We'll give you the woods, up to the bridge in the east," I pause, "and deliver tribute from the lowlands. Monthly. Half of the reap."

"What?" Astonished, the Captain draws his sword, pointing the end at my chest.

"You traitor," the mace wielder mutters under his breath. I grab the end of the blade wielded in betrayal, pulling it into my breastplate. One of the edges finds its way between my gauntlet, drawing blood from the bottom of my palm, soaking the water with the thick red substance.

"Listen to me. This is it, do you understand? We're out of time, we were always out of time," I look back at Zegruth, eyeing us as we argue softly, the ogres closing in, insistent stomps, One, Two, One, Two, One, Two, closer and closer, louder, inside me, inside my chest, "You two fend off the goblins at our backs, Nestor and I will combat Zegruth and the hobgoblins. Signal to the bowman he must target the ogres, they may yet become our allies in a rampage."

"Yes sir," the Captain holds out his right hand, moving his fingers in a code only they know. Would they betray me once again, striking me in the back with an arrow as soon as they get the chance? Bargaining with the beast himself? It can't be. It cannot. Louder. A roar. The goblins disperse, the ogres destroying the recently evacuated land. We are out of time.

"Zegruth!" I draw my sword and offer it to the sky, "I, the Prince of Amiens, Warrior of the Phoenix and Liberator of Light, will show you the wrath of the gods, will claim your head for meddling in the affairs of my kingdom. Draw your weapon! And face thee fate!"

"It is so," the beast retrieves its weapon from a few of the goblins who haul the massive spear, one with three prongs and a heavy handle of solid steel. The tips appear more black than the sky which had become storm ridden. The wind is even stronger now and I struggle to keep my sword straight in the air. The downpour begins now, slow and light but I feel the water hitting my hair, wetting my scalp. The bugbear howls and the shouting of goblins follows. They begin their charge.

"Nestor on me!" I shout to him as I steady my stance in the ever increasing current which carries parts of myself away by the second. We have to stay in the water. The red water that pools around me. I've drawn first blood and we've yet to meet.

"Yes sir," he moves just next to me, elbows clashing. Both our breaths rapid and short.

"I'm sorry I couldn't save you."

"Your chance is still to come."

CRUSH THEM

A scream from behind. There is no time to see. No time to think. On my right arrows fly by, the zip of air passing overhead. Metal on metal, edges tearing skin, ripping leather. The beast strides directly at my blade. In two steps it stands before me, and in one swing the sword in Nestor's hand is flung back. Thrown off balance he falls into the water. The three pronged spear aimed in his direction, I let go of the downward pressure keeping my feet steady and slide in front of his flailing body. Just barely my blade catches the prongs, a ringing reverberates through my arms and up into my skull. Without a beat the beast passes the spear to his other hand, flipping the shaft end toward my unprotected head. Again by luck, and with the support of both my gauntlets on the tang of my shaking sword, the wood crashes and slides off with a flash of light. The beast jumps back to poise for another strike.

An ogre roars closer than any of the previous calls, the sound of one of their metal chains slamming into the ground, bones crushing, splatter of water from the brook. An arrow hits a goblin near me, striking its throat, curdling blood bubbles in breathless struggle. The rain pours heavier, partially obscuring my vision. Nestor is back on his feet a few paces behind me, ready to defend. The spear reaches along the surface of the rushing water, spraying into my face, Nestor swings down onto the prongs, pinning them under the water as I let the current carry me. A hand on my arm. A big hand. Club to the face, blood streaks down into my eyes, or from my eyes. The club swings again before I see where it came from, crushing the armor over my stomach, half the air knocked out of me, I stab in a random pattern on my right, the end gets stuck in something. I swing my left arm over and connect with the face of a hobgoblin. His massive, rough hand grips my jaw and forces me under the water, holding my head to the riverbed. I reach for anything, wet, metal hands sliding off his skin, my skull is going to explode, the pressure is too much. Fading. My sword. My hand finds the blade still implanted in his body, the edge burns into my skin as I tighten around it, ripping the sword away and viciously swinging above me. For a moment his hold on my head relaxes, I slash at his arm and let the water carry me even further. Water in my lungs, water in my eyes, in my head.

I stand and find myself far away from the battle. I can't see much, blood and water flooding my vision. Screaming, rumbling in the air, in the ground, iron chimes, lightning cracking. Nestor. Where is Nestor. I can hardly move, the current pushes me back with every step I attempt. I slide my sword into where the scabbard at my hip should be, but it's gone. Tossing the sword onto the shore, I begin unstrapping my armor. I need to become lighter. I let the water carry the pieces away. The cold water touches my skin more easily, filling my every pore if there were any that remained free to this moment, though it feels as if so. I jump and paddle and push myself to land, on my hands and knees breathing heavily. I spit out a mixture of thick, sour blood, runny water, and stomach juice. I hack it up, handfuls pouring out with each gust entering my throat.

"I thought you might last a little longer," I raise my head to the sight of Zegruth walking along the brook, spear blooded.

"I'm not done yet," I barely eke out the words before launching into a coughing fit, blood everywhere. I reach for my sword and can barely grasp it, the skin on my right hand is almost entirely sheared off, bone peering through the muscle. I grab the hilt with my left, pushing off the ground. I stand face to face with the beast.

"Brave, but you've lost everything. Where's your armor? Your men? Your crown, *prince*?" My crown. Atop my head is nothing but soaked hair. It laughs at me, cackling, long teeth thrashing about.

"I need nothing but my heart and soul," though I know that is a lie. The crown was the only connection I had left, the only thing keeping me royal, exalted, strong. The power flowed into my body from its glisten, the power bestowed upon me by the gods. And now it lies far downstream, forever lost. Maybe it was always lost.

"Allow me to retrieve those for you," just as before, the beast takes his long strides, closing the distance in a mere second or two. A flash of lightning illuminates the prongs moving at my chest. My sword slides between two of the prongs, the third grazing my collarbone. Zegruth pushes harder, unable to use my second hand; the third prong moves deeper under my skin. I feel the bone cracking, the surface splintering into my chest. I slide the sharp tip upward, slicing just below the dark eyes focused on my blood. Its strength gives, I pivot to force my back at the water. I may need it to escape once again.

The spear swings at hip level as if to slash across my body with the long, sharp cones. With ease I deflect both swings which come, the first followed by a second much quicker, shallower one. The third comes as a stab, I know I can only block two prongs. Down on one knee I force the swing to come at an angle, the third prong unable to reach me. A furry fist beats on my chest, I fall to both knees. The thick handle hits the side of my neck, vision out for a few seconds, another bone cracking sound, thick liquid soaks my already water logged clothing. I can't move. The prongs fly toward my stomach, the same motion Nestor saved me from earlier. Nestor. Where is Nestor. The tips pierce my skin. Cold and quick. They tear through my innards, out the skin of my back, splitting my spine. I'm lifted off my feet, body limp, held up to the sky. My head falls down to the right, the muscle torn, hanging on by the thin skin wrapped around what threads are left.

Zegruth laughs. It stares into my eyes, laughing, mouth wide open, yellow, nauseating teeth in motion. The thick tongue reaches out of its mouth, the abrasive surface swirling around my flaccid face. I can hardly smell, but the saliva coagulates in my every orifice, a fish and egg odor, if my body could vomit it would. The blood oozing out of my neck wound is licked up, the inside of my mouth drained of its own saliva, its tongue rubbing my teeth, into the back of my throat, down my wretched, torn esophagus. In one motion I am swung away and down, into the water, straight on my back. I land on the riverbed, water entering my body, and close my eyes.

March 14

Whence things have their origin,
there too they must pass according to necessity;
for they must pay penalty and be judged for their injustice,
according to the ordinance of
time.
-Anaximander or Simplicius (or I)

Face up on the platform, I stare straight at the stars - of which there are none. The leaves block out any light which could be there, though there is no evidence that the night brings any. No wind, no movement, no noise, why should there be light? So I cannot see much, but my eyes have finally adjusted to the darkness. It's about time. As I go to sit up I find there is no strength left in my frail body. Where was I? The platform is no longer moving, I turn my head side to side, searching for the lever as if I could reach it. It stands on my right, snapped in half like a pencil. Now I see the platform itself is splintered, broken into pieces, the crates missing, the bodies nowhere in sight. I lay on the wood chunk alone, on my back, unable to move. A howl in the distance. Another two follow. Further away. I grab onto a protruding piece of wood and pull myself away from the edge, expecting my legs to swing up, but there is nothing. I gather the strength to lift my head, just enough to eclipse my chest, and see nothing. In place of my lower body there is only darkness. My head slams down onto the hard surface. With my free hand I slowly probe where my stomach should be. Slime, tubes, fibrous material inflating and deflating, I grab onto it and feel the flexible mesh, further down I run my fingers along my severed spine, the rigid bones threatening to split open my delicate palm. Using both hands now I pull further up the platform, my exposed organs scraping against the jagged wood below me. I reach the half lever, take a deep, moist breath, and with the last of my energy I slide off the platform face first into the water below.

March 15

The fluid engulfs my cheeks, swarming my entire head, flowing over the rest of my body. I've fallen into a shallow pond it seems. I can feel the air touching my back, only I lie face down, nose in the wet dirt. Finally, I can drown in peace. Simply let go of what life I have left. It should be quick. Only then can I rest. I breathe the water in, struggling through the mask the soil formed over my nostrils. It burns my lungs but I force it down, opening my throat as wide as I can, sucking in more and more. Vibrations in the water alert me to the presence of another, approaching quickly. They slosh in a careless manner, the underwater current hitting me in the face. Hands on the back of my shirt, I am lifted out of the water, only my upper body as my legs hang bent at the waist. With sunken, tired eyes I peer up at whatever plucked me so easily. Long, thick brown hair, devilish green eyes, charming smile: The Captain?

"Is it really you?" Water drops out of my mouth, my voice strained.

"Aye," his smile grows even larger, "seems I arrived in the nick of time."

I force a slight smile as he throws me over his shoulder. The sun hangs high in the sky, burning my exposed skin and already drying the layer of water that coated my entire body. All I can see is water, calm, light blue water, all the way to the horizon. The sound of a bustling group grows as his steps grow less liquidy, crunching on leaves, occasionally resonating on lacquered wood. Boxes and rope and heavy metal? They are moving lots of equipment, disorganized and haphazard, it's being thrown around.

"Id you find im in the bay again?" A tall, bald man with more bones than muscle runs alongside my dangling body, examining my face as if I were an exotic animal. The Captain did not respond. His steps remain steady.

"How much you drink last night?" Another man, sturdy and dressed in loose burlap pants and what appears to be a shirt made from a worn out quilt, follows behind us now. He reaches up to my face with his thick fingers, raising my eyelids so far I thought my eyes might slip out.

"I don't know," they burst into laughter. I keep shifting my head aside but his fingers always follow, toying with my face like a child. Whatever. I am too tired to do anything about it.

"Have you two finished the rigging?" The ground below is solid now, planks upon planks, a platform. No. Miniature waves splash the sides, large white birds caw overhead, groaning wood, a dock.

"Of course Captain," in unison they stand up straight, filing across the bridge into the underbelly of the tall, mahogany ship. Still limp, I am carried under the arch behind them. All the light is gone in an instant, even squinting I can hardly make out the features of the room. A few rickety chairs off to one side, thin lumber pillars about, oil lamps hanging off them, empty metal cages, cracked barrels overflowing with grain and slimy fish, and a low ceiling flexing under the hundreds of footsteps rumbling above. I blink rapidly, wiping my eyes with the back of my hand only to receive a sightful of sand. I wince and let my body fall loose. There is no point in doing anything. I only cause my own pain. Again and again. Please just let me go to sleep.

I am startled, twitching in mid air, as I am swung - thrown almost - from the shoulder of the Captain, his hands on my waist, onto a grouping of leather sacks in the far corner of the hall. He turns and waltzes back toward the entrance, his tall boots slapping against the floor boards. Immediately I am swarmed by the two idiots from before, along with three more that seem to have spawned from thin air. My head wobbles from side to side, I feel more dizzy now that I am stationary, or maybe it is the slight rocking of the boat, but my eyes hurt, pressure wells in my forehead.

"What's wrong wit im?"

"I'm fucking drunk," I groan, bile reaches the back of my throat but I force it down in a dry gulp. The group howls with laughter, throwing their heads back, cackling like no other.

"Your drunk mate? You know were s'pposed a sail today?"

"No, I didn't," oh god, my body feels like it will drift away, up into the air and leave behind my eyes, heavy and swirling.

"Well good luck! Captn says storms ahead."

"One of yous is gonna ave to watch im."

"I already got sweeps."

"No way in hell."

"Sorry mate but yer on your own."

They pat each other on the back, smiling as if they came up with the world's greatest idea. Slowly meandering away from my near lifeless body, the lanky one grabs a sack full of various fruits, tossing them to each of the buffoons. An apple hits me in the side of the head, not hard enough to hurt ,but again I am startled as I jump out of my skin. With that they chuckle and leave out the arched door, I guess I did not give them the reaction they wanted. Alone I lie, sprawled on the tanned leather, an apple in my lap, and nothing else to my name. Conversations buzz above: men yelling and women laughing, drums banging and strings vibrating a swift melody, wood scraping on the roof as someone pushes a crate from one end to the other, small wheels rolling along - all in another world.

So far removed. How did I end up here? Drunk, useless, alone. In the brig unable to even lift my head. I'm supposed to be a leader, yet the example I set is one no one can follow, no one wants to follow. Who would want to be me? Not even I. Here in the dank, lonely hall, I wish I could be someone else, somewhere else. Why here? Why me? Is living not enough, must I always be aware of my incompetence, feel the guilt of the facade of success? I grab the apple and bring it to my mouth, my head completely limp on the sacks, and sink my teeth into the skin. They slice through the squishy, luke warm innards - I hate overripe apples. One bite and I throw the dull fruit to the side. Why me?

"Are you gonna come to the embark speeches? You already missed the first one," a woman with hair like silk stands in the doorway.

"Can you help me up?" I manage to raise my head enough to make eye contact with her. She smiles and jogs toward me, offering her entire shoulder under my arm, hers wrapped around my back.

"What happened to you? You're not just drunk... are you?"

"No. I got fucked up."

"Oh?" We hobble between the boxes and barrels randomly placed in the hall, careful to avoid the thick braided ropes laying about.

"Like you wouldn't believe."

"I'm sure of that, never seen you look worse."

"Thanks."

"You know what I mean," she giggles and raises me a little, I was sliding away from her grasp. Holding my body up still seems like the most difficult task ever, my legs hardly receiving the input I so intensely focus on.

"How long was I gone?"

"Last I saw you was three nights ago, before you went out with Cap and the others."

"Ah."

"Yea. No wonder, huh?"

"Why didn't you stop me?" I smile and turn my head toward her, looking up at her face. She rolls her eyes.

"I tried but you just don't listen."

"Well next time make me," we reach the bottom of the ramp up to the main deck and she slips out from under me, grabbing my hands in hers and dragging me along the slope. My feet struggle to keep up, flailing to remain on the ground. She lets out a sweet, throaty laugh. I can't help but laugh too, eyes open. I feel better already.

"Gladly," the fresh air hits my face in a strong gust, forcing breath into my nostrils. Everyone stands in a huddled mass just below the pedestal housing the wheel and ladder to the perch, where a man delivers a speech. Every few words, cheers erupt from the crowd. The clapping is constant, someone whistles in support, a drum beats in unison with the cheers, rumbling into the beginnings of each sentence. We stop and lean on the rails along the side of the ship, rocking back and forth, the soft waves splash droplets into my face. She hollers right next to my ear, the pitch jarring. I shove her and she hits me on the back of the head. Damn.

"You know my head still hurts," I mutter through my teeth.

"Sorry," clearly not, she smiles and goes back to her unruly cheering. I look up to the pedestal where Brigs stands, I was not paying attention to when he started, but he is close to finishing now as he trails off, speaking of whatever comes to his mind. Someone should take his place. This is embarrassing.

"Maria, if I never come back, I love you," he cries out into the sky, voice cracking all the while.

"She's not here you idiot!" A few laughs.

"Aye, only wish she was."

"I too, for her taste lingers in my mouth," everyone is sent into an uproar, some laugh and some begin yelling at each other.

"What?" Brigs leaps over the railing, "Rick, you bastard!" She and I are far enough to be saved from the festivities, but the ensuing fight moves uncomfortably close. Brigs grabs Rick by the collar and throws him across the deck, a shoving fight breaks out and one of the fat men who was bothering me earlier lands at our feet. She picks him up by the shoulders and pushes him back toward the fight, laughing and cheering him on.

"How many speeches did we get through?" I slide my arm into hers, guiding her along the side of the deck.

"Two and a half, unfortunately."

"Whoever let Brigs go third is an idiot."

"Is that so?" I had been looking at her since we started walking, but I look up to see the Captain standing atop the stairs of which we were about to climb. He smiles and offers his arm to lock with my free one, mockingly of course. She propels off me, lunging up the stairs in two steps. Before I can step up one of the brawlers falls into me, back to back we slam into the stairs, his weight crushing me, sweat dripping onto my cheek, creeping into my mouth. My face is in the stair, but I can hear another man approaching. They're going to crush me.

"Get off me " I shout to no avail. I can feel the burly hands wrap around the neck of the man above me, his fingernails brushing the back of my neck. Oh god, we will both suffocate at the hands of one man. God damn Brigs. Damn this ship. I should've stayed below deck. After all I've been through only to die on the helmsman's stairs. The cracked, stale wood the last thing I will ever see, so close I could get splinters in my eye. It smells of freshly salted meat, or maybe it's the sweat, or my final dream. I hear someone yell above, it must be the Captain but I cannot tell. All I can make out is the heavy grunts of the man sitting on my spine, his throat close to my ear, squishy, wet gusts of air struggle out. Again the Captain yells. My eyelids are becoming heavy, the last wisps of air leave my lungs, my throat tightens. A fist hits the side of my head. Why me?

A gunshot rings through the air and the fighting sounds come to an abrupt halt. One more crash of wood and a sharp yelp come from behind me. But, the fat man is lifted off my back. I turn over and gasp for air, the cool breeze rushes into my mouth, its saltiness coating my tongue. If only. I throw my head back onto a stair and look to the sky. The sun had lowered a considerable amount, leaving rough, sullen clouds in its place. I can almost see the water from here. Water above and water below. Where is it not? If only I could escape. It will surely rain before we depart and judging by the height of the wispy masses, it will rain for long after. We must leave lest we remain here forever. She will not take pity on us, nor will she relent for we have not yet begun. I am sorry Gaia, so deeply sorry. I will set them on track. Please, just a few moments more. Give me your strength and I will show you our worth. I promise. A bout of thunder shakes the planks below me, the threatening sound reaching into my ears and shaking both my inside and out. I smile, blowing a kiss into the empty air. She is somewhere here, her grace is mine. My chance has arrived. Finally.

The Captain had been speaking to the crew, but clearly they care not for his antics. I spring up and make my way to the pedestal where Brigs had been, and the Captain now stands. Placing my hand on his shoulder, I pull him toward me, my face mere inches from his, I can feel the air leaving his mouth as he speaks. His brow questions me.

"Let me," I wink and smile just as he did when he saved me, it is my turn now, "I know what to do."

"Of course," he moves aside and down one step to my left. I come to the rail that overlooks the deck, shattered barrels lie about, divots in the deck where the fattest of men had landed, the sail of the fore-mast -

draped over the rail - flaps in the wind, bruised and bleeding faces peer at me, waiting. Waiting for what? They know not. They could never know, never understand what it means to know. Yet, I must explain to them as my life depends on it. Not my living life, but the life that is worth living, if they cannot understand, why am I here? Now is my chance.

"Hello everyone," a few grumbles cross the crowd, "first things first, we've got ourselves a lot of work to do, looking at you Brigs. Wherever ye are you fucked us. Anyhow, we must leave before the storm hits. As you all know embarking in a storm means a risk of grounding and we will most definitely sink in this weather, so we will work into the night. Second," I am scanning the crowd and my eyes land upon her face, she is wincing for me. Right, what am I saying? I'm a fucking idiot, "does everyone know why we're here? Does anyone know why?"

I slide along the rail, pacing from side to side: "We came from all over the world, some of us twice so, to be here. In this very boat, in this very bay, on this wary eve. Under the helm of *the,* Captain. To sail this ship, the masterfully constructed oak beauty, la Malattia, together!, against our once forgotten foe. It is under the banner of camaraderie we sail, to face our enemy, and yet we face each other, toe to toe with your brother, why?" I pause for a moment, looking to the sky where the clouds twirl as if a funnel prepares to pour them into our berth, "Because we lost sight of what it means to be, a man," her eyes, "or woman - what it means to be a sailor. To gather in a pile of wood and cross the ocean which only wants us dead, to realize we enjoy the treachery, thrive in the intensity and joy of being abroad, alone with each other. Nothing but us, the boat, the sky, and the water which gives us life. It is, after all, the only thing that is real. So. For the boat! And our brothers, and the Captain, we sail!"

A couple of cheers and only one sad clap from her small hands: "We sail in this cursed boat, cursed because we are on it, cursed because it was built, we sail on it for it is cursed, otherwise the ship is no more than wood and nails. The curse guides us and calls for its own destruction! We, the sailors, the men - and woman - must fight this curse. It lives in the boards below our feet, writhing through the splinters, rippling in the wind swept sails, it wraps our bodies and clouds our minds. Clearly! We have yet to sail, and we sail all the same! Assailants against another, against yourself! We are together, we must be. We must act together, sail as one, one ship, one crew, one enemy, *the* enemy. It is our duty as sailors!"

The whistling is back, loud whistling and cheers from the crowd. I can hear her voice, her yells peculiar and harsh, striking my ears along with the rumbling of sailor feet and fleshy applause. The Captain puts his arm around me and looks out over the crew. He smiles. I did it. We did it. Now is our time. Now. It is the only time, and it is mine. Ours. His hair brushes my cheek in the wind, the soft ends tickling the surface of my skin. It carries his scent as well, surprisingly strong enough to overcome the salt and wetness descending from the clouds, nature in my nose and him in my mouth. He smells of cedar; like walking through the woods on the second week of spring. He reminds me of someone...

"Now is our time!" As if he read my mind his voice pushes against my ear, out into the air, flowing over the deck. He raises his free arm into the air, hand balled into a fist. "Now is our time!"

Now is our time!

They shout in unison, chanting almost. The storm hovers above us now, joining in the chant with a voice of its own, a raucous roar. I feel within me a roar, though it remains inside threatening to break free, yet cautious, for its demise lies in being free. One who spends their entire life in search of freedom has but one goal, and once quenched, what is one to do? Is there a freedom more free than being free? The sail which had been torn down in the scuffle flies in the air, attached to the mast only by its bottom corner with a knot so loose now it could fly away. It flutters in the wind, the increasingly angry wind, as if she holds onto one end and forces the ripples herself. I did what you asked of me. Why are you still angry? Why then do you force the storm upon me? Can I not be calm in these moments, can I relax when all is said and done? Is it not done now? Lightning strikes down on the land before me and a boom follows, so loud my eyes jolt in their socket. We need to leave. We must press on.

"Let's get to work," I say softly to the Captain.

"Why don't you tell them yourself?" I raise my brow in question, a slight smile hits my face. "I know."

He lets go of me, moving to the rail: "Let's get to work! Everyone on deck, sailors to duty, we leave when the sun touches the horizon."

Yes sir!

The men bustle to life, like ants leaving the hill they scramble to clear the ruin above. The Captain too. He vaults the rail as Brigs did, his heavy boots landing with a crack not unlike that of the lightning, and begins issuing orders, tossing fabrics and pieces of wood to the men who find little purpose. Others tie the fore-sail back on straight, adjusting the bottom knot meanwhile; some begin the sweeping and scrubbing, their arms in a wild swing to cover as much ground as possible. I see them, but the sounds of their toil seem so distant, as if the stairs are tenfold in number, the rail a barrier overlooking the cliff. Maybe the air separates us, high on my perch it swirls all around, carrying away the sounds like a stream does rocks. Or it is me, might I feel far away, distant, because I want it to be so? Or rather, I want so badly not to be that I cannot help but force a rift, the world on one side and I on the other. She pushes me away the more I pull. But I cannot let her come to me on her own accord, for she surely would not if I showed no desire for her arrival. So what is it then? Am I wrong? So wrong that I am like no other, and no other alike I, never wishing to be anything like me, why would they? I stand above the crew, not as their superior, but as their watcher. I watch and see and try to hear but I cannot, try to feel but I cannot. And, in this watching, I see the emptiness within about. Everywhere in every one, every thing, I see me - which could not be more unalike that which is real.

"He didn't give you anything to do?"

"No."

"I'm surprised," she climbs the stairs like a gull skims the surface, gliding straight to me. She stops one pace away, so quickly her scent, like his did, reaches me in a short gust.

"I've never been one for work."

"Is that so?"

"Yes," I look into her eyes and see nothing. They are blue with wrinkles in the color, crevices that create the illusion of texture, small eyes, but nothing. I look into them and see nothing, they are there, two eyes, two balls of spongy membrane, two circles with color in them, but there is nothing to them. They are just eyes, they are not her's, they live in the body which she also lives in, allowing her to see outside-

"What's wrong with you?"

"I don't know."

"Seriously, I'm asking. You still seem off."

"How so?" She blinks and moves away from me, leaning on the rail overlooking the sea. She does not respond. Instead, she stares into the opaque water. The waves lap against the curved wood of the boat, they wash over each other, bubbles forming in their wake, that soft splashing sound...

"I think this will be my last voyage," she is still.

"But you love the sea, the openness, the freedom," I look at her but she does not move, either ignoring my intense eyes or absent altogether.

"I do," she pauses for a while, her breaths deep and pulsing, yet soft, "but sometimes it's the worst thing in the world."

"It can't always be perfect."

"What if something else can?"

"Nothing is perfect," I reach out, my hand about to touch her shoulder. She pulls away, her head turns in a sharp, startling motion.

"What if I want to try?" We both look at the other's face, waiting, for what? Is there anything either of us could say, anything we should say? It's not the words that matter, it's who is saying them.

I smile: "Then you know where to find me, for anything, send for me and I'll drop everything. If it means you can be happy."

"I might be."

"And if not you can always come back," she leans on the rail again, looking toward the horizon this time. The sun inches closer and closer to its rest, it is almost time. I laugh to myself.

"Return?"

"Yes."

"If only it were possible"

"It has to be, there is no reason for it not to be," the sounds of work and rigging and scrubbing and singing slow down, they fade into the air, into the sounds of the sky, or what is below the sky and above us, it must be below for it harbors an infinite expanse only I can see. The clouds are loud, their electricity slips between the wisps, occasionally falling to our land, the land below. I feel a few drops, small ones, patter on my bare skin. So small, yet so wet.

"Only time will tell."

"If it could speak, it might protest."

"We will see," she rolls her eyes, "is that better?"

"No, but it's okay," the slapping of thick heels approaches from the stairway.

"Did you two even pretend to help?"

"No," we recite in unison.

"Of course not," his smile reveals two rows of teeth, aligned but uneven in length. Everything stands still for a moment too long, the wind pretends to pause, the rain ceases to fall, I do not move and neither does she, his mouth remains open, not even twitching in the slightest, our eyes blinkless, motionless, staring, I cannot remember if I took a breath but my lungs did not complain. In this moment, nothing occurred, yet everything possible happened all at once. The entirety of the world flashed before us and faded against our strongest wishes. It was a moment I knew not of its existence, I only saw the Captain, his teeth, the dark oak wood behind him, and dark active sky above him, but it was here. Or maybe we were not here, transported to the world and back, to see for just a moment.

I break the repose: "Are we ready?"

"I suppose so," I look to the horizon, the sun dipping its toes into the water.

"Should we not be gone already?"

"If only," he skips the steps to the helm. In one motion he finds himself in command of the wheel, feet apart and head high. He issues a few commands and the ship is readied, the dock sliding away from its place at our side. She comes to my side and leans her head on my shoulder. We watch the Captain in his spot, his place, the only place he could be, he should be. If only we could fall into place too.

"Do you think the storm will be bad?" She asks even though her knowledge of this sea far surpasses anyone else aboard. I tilt my head up, seeing the clouds once more. They still swirl, as if the lead chases the lagging, much heavier one; but, the static stopped - no lightning, no thunder.

"Yes."

"Why's that?"

"I just do."

She nods on my shoulder and we say no more.

The Late Evening of March 15

The sun was long gone, not to return for days to come. It will certainly hide behind the clouds that stretch from horizon to horizon, enjoying its game of hide and seek all the while. Giggling and pointing at us from behind the veil, the sun will feel joy in these days. For now, she fell below the covers on which we rest in unrest, for they move in waves like a flag in the wind - in the strong wind, and we feel each ripple more than a fabric could. I can hardly sleep as every few waves we are lifted into the air by the air, force of the waves, and my body is flung from side to side, colliding with the curved oak wall I lay next to in hopes that it might impede my movement. It does not. But, the comfort of knowing the wall is my only enemy far outweighs my disappointment. To be in the midst of those sweat covered hoodlums, I would not.

"You're awake?" In the darkness my eyes struggle to make out what figure stands before me, the only light comes from the far end of the hall, but the jumping flame illuminates an unmistakable head of wavy, brown tinged hair.

"I can hardly sleep."

"What's new?"

"Well it's worse tonight," he walks over and sits beside me, our backs to the wall, heads resting on the planks. We are careful not to relax in full, one irregular wave and we may bash the back of our skulls.

"It doesn't look like it'll pass for at least another day."

"I would say two."

"I was trying to be optimistic."

"Optimism won't help me sleep."

"It does nothing for me either yet I still tried."

"As you should," he smiles and breathes out as if to signal a quiet laugh. His hands brush his hair back, moving the front behind his ears and running over the rest. His eyes look to me but his head is unmoved, he waits for me to say something more, "I was talking to Lila earlier."

"While you were supposed to be working?"

"Yes," a grin hits my face, "she got me thinking though,"

"About what?"

"If you'd wait I would tell you - I'm trying to make it dramatic," he laughs and nods, bringing his knees to his chest and cradling his legs, "this is her last voyage you know?"

He raises his brow as if he already knew, and says nothing.

"It's just... I never really had a choice," he raises his other brow, "I went along with everything I was supposed to and ended up here." I am not sure there is anything else to say, could there be anything else than this? "Don't get me wrong, I love it here! But is it really what I wanted?"

"What would you have done instead?"

"I don't know," I pause for a moment and take a breath, "I do know, but it's stupid, and there's no way."

"If it was your dream it's not stupid," his face turns serious, concerned even.

"I think there's a difference between dreams and goals; that's why they're called dreams."

"A man who does not dream is no man at all," he reaches out and touches my cheek with the back of his hand, the skin rough but touch softer than the most delicate petals of a lily, "How else would he become anything, let alone a man?"

"True, imagination is indeed the basis for life. Yet, imagination is to imaginary as dreams are to sleep, the antithesis to awake, to life."

"Do you ever sleep?"

"Hardly, I do dream, however."

"Dream, or imagine?"

"Dream. Sometimes, when I manage to feel asleep, I see things I do not think of. I think them but I do not think of them. Only then do I dream of adventure, of being important, of feeling something other than how I am supposed to feel," he is intensely focused on me now, it seems as if the world has stopped around us once more, the waves stuck in place, the boat tilted back mid-climb, "When I was young, not much younger than I am now, but certainly young, I dreamt of being a knight or a noble, maybe. To travel the world, dispatching evil and reveling in the good, everyone looking at me like I am I, like I am *the* someone. To be powerful and use that power for the benefit of those who lack *my* power. I know now it was just my imagination, a child's hopes, for I am not strong, or powerful, or important, and most definitely not good. I only live these things in my sleep, the moment between life and death where dreams bridge the gap. In the back of my mind I still wish I could be, but I know it is not possible. In my pursuit of dreams, I will forget what it means to live, but is that life worth living if my dreams are not realized?"

"Is it better to live in despair or waste life in false hope," he frowns, knowing he sees what I have seen all along. I nod and lower my eyes.

"I think I might go too."

"With her?"

"No, somewhere I can be free."

"Only if such a place exists."

"Whether I find it or not, I will start anew."

"Free from now."

"Precisely, only a fool believes he can be free from the restraints of the world, but nothing holds me from moving side to side across land or sea."

"And that you shall," a long break enters our conversation and my eyes begin to droop. It is late. He reaches over and puts his arm around me, his hand gripping my side, and pulls me down to his lap. His hand slides over my neck, into my hair, the nails scratching my lonely scalp. I close my eyes and forget where I am. I may as well be somewhere safe, the Captain massaging my head and comforting me to a deep slumber, somewhere with soft grass and flowers as far as the eye can see and a multitude of stars above illuminating the tender scenery. I only wish I was. Instead, we rock back and forth in the bottom of this cursed boat, the boat which threatens to take our lives, yet gives them motion. He whispers as not to disturb my resting process: "You know I too dream. Of flying."

"Flying?" I say from the brink of sleep.

"Yes, flying, like a bird. Sailing is close enough, gliding across the water feels something similar I would imagine, but the ability to glide over land and sea both? That feeling is unmatched."

"It is freedom too, you seek?"

"Peace."

"If only we had wings."

March 16

I stand at the podium overlooking a meager crowd, the hall is rather large and my audience sits sparse, spread out like the sheep of a poorly managed herd. Each wall adorns long felt blocks the color of northern tree leaves, spaced evenly and shaped to captivate the sound, all sound. I hear them murmuring among themselves, whispering over my speech, just as loud as my own voice bouncing off the far wall and slanted ceiling. In this moment I pause to allow my eyes their freedom to wander, each person looks back at me, but we do not look at each other - it is because I am here that they present themselves, that presence bringing my absence. Why do they not care? Why should they avoid listening to the words I have spoken? The words that mean nothing and everything, the words that are for all and for none, is there not one I am meant to be?

"Excuse me!" A voice comes from below, closer to the edge of the stage than I perceived any audience member would be, perhaps I had paused for a moment too long, perhaps I should not have paused at all for a moment is far too long yet all too short, perhaps the moment is this moment and in this moment I speak.

"Yes sir," I answer confidently.

"May I ask a question?"

"A second question."

"Third, truly," they quip back as I had hoped and I smile, a little laugh leaving my nose. I nod:

"Go ahead."

"A long time ago, not so long ago that you would have forgotten, but just long enough that the memory has begun to fade, I sat across from you and asked for your assistance."

"A past student of mine," I state but ask.

"Student and good friend, some would say the best, most intimate friend."

"Of course. How could I forget."

"You could not."

"And yet I began to."

"As you must. No thing remains forever."

"If only."

"I would advise against it," he speaks these words and I look around, still no one pays attention to me, now us. We speak to each other and they speak among themselves, entirely oblivious to the conversation taking place just in front of them. The conversation so loud and bold, important and unheard, isolated in this grand hall. I was to speak to the audience, but I now speak with an audience as if it is only us, alone in this hall, grand, luxurious hall.

"I missed you."

"May I ask my question now?"

"Have you not already?" I pause to see the lights, a ring of metal with illuminated glass hanging down from smaller rings in its midst, like a star I see rays peeling off the center of each shard, the longer I stare the closer it feels. I bring my eyes down, "it feels so long ago."

"I did once. But I wish to again."

"I wish many things."

"I suppose it makes little difference."

"I suppose not."

"Will you read your first work, or, the work you first read to me years ago?"

"And which one would that be?"

"I know not the name, but what it was about."

"I see. Of course I'll read it for you, and anyone who should listen."

"Even I should not, yet I will."

"Let it be so," I sort through my papers sitting atop the podium, I know it is here somewhere. I need not the paper, but it feels good in my hands, to see and feel the sheet as I read. Finally, I may do what I came here for, I may speak and be heard - if only for a moment. I look into his eyes, his spirited, watching eyes, and begin so:

Whence I was born,
there too I found my place
in the origin which precedes all origins -
if I have not yet been born, who then am I?
Hence I was born,
and there my place decided
not by I, but for me, with I.
Yet things are unsatisfied,
they cry for more,
reach for that which belongs to them,
belonging due to the desire for its place
not for it has place
as that was already decided,
yet things are unsatisfied.
They beg for more,
cry out "is it unjust that I am no more than me?"
grasp that which "belongs" to them,
it feels at home in their hands,

73

their hands which they love, which they know best, their rough hands,
nails filled with silt -
grimy, bone ringed things,
they grip onto it like their life depends on it.
It does not.
They may hold the future's waist
but the closer they swing toward its presence,
the sooner a return to the origin shows itself,
there, every thing is satisfied -
yet all things are unsatisfied.
They do not know who they are,
always wish to be something else,
they fall to their knees, scrounge for all they can,
and when there is no thing left they simply take more.
Hence I was born:

sunken eyes, clouds hang low
salt water drops from high
is it mine? or am I in tow
blown along with dewy wisps,
Who am I to know?

I look up to see those eyes unmoved, those eyes that match no other. In them I see what I have always seen, and through them I see what will never be seen by another but I. To hold such eyes is to be. So few are given the chance, so few I would believe none, the chance to see beyond one's own sight - to be. Yet, less is all I will know, and for that I am grateful. Why waste time being when I can watch just as well? Would it not be a waste of mine own eyes in refusing to see from within my skull, scorned to look upon and never into? But his eyes are this way, as if the wet, soft balls can see in all directions, his sight spherical and so he sees around. He looks at me, his pupils piercing my heart, listening to my every word, but he sees others. He need not look at anything in particular, why waste time seeing when he can watch just as well? Watching all and none, simultaneously and at no time at all. There is no time to watch, only now and forever, but most importantly never. Where is time in seeing if one does not speak of when?

"Hey," he speaks rather aggressively. My eyes refocus:

"Yes," my mind is still elsewhere, my eyes far too weak to see anything other than his.

"This is it, the end."

"Of?"

"Our moment."

"I thought it had already ended," I say, even though I did not think it.

"Rather it has just begun."

"Yet we are at the end all the same."

"How can one begin if there is no end?"

"I suppose they can't."

"I suppose not," he leaps up onto the stage, so graceful his arms flow by his side, landing just before me. He places his hand on my chest, just below my neck, and speaks into me, "Our moment has lasted a bit too long I'm afraid."

"If I could go back, back to before, I would never have left."

"Oh you can, just not with I in tow," his unmoved eyes face their first complication, tears well above his lower eyelid, threatening to fall over the ledge.

"Why then would I choose to return if you will not be present?"

"In my absence I am present, I will be present always for I never left, and always absent for I never came. How could I come when I am already here?"

"And so you will never come?" Now my eyes fill with tears, except they do not hold themselves back. Drops fall so rapidly my shirt becomes soaked in two rows, the sound of the drops splattering on his skin comes from below, and my vision blurs from the excess waves.

"Precisely."

"I'll miss you."

"I already have, and forever will miss you. Not now, but forever."

"And never."

We speak in unison: "For now is no time at all, I love you and that is all."

For a moment I think he will not go, he can not. What will I do without him but everything I have always done? No matter what I think, he must go. I just wish he would not. I wish we could exist as whoever whenever doing whatever, our place never decided nor told to us. But it must be, it always has been since before and after - he is gone. Before my eyes he slips away into the air inhabiting the lonely, sweeping hall. I can almost see his wisps in the stars of light, intensifying their rays into spots of shine. My eyes linger, wishing to see a wisp just once more, only once more, but the light does no more than burn its imprint into my sight. I close my eyes and raise my arms above my head, reaching for that which is not there, reaching for nothing and everything - if only my arms were big enough to hold such a thing.

I open my eyes and the fire looms over all. They were not closed for all that long, yet I am alone in the hall once again, standing among the flames. The warmth is beautiful. The licks of fire grab at my skin, burning my surface with their fingertips. I will die. I am to die. Yet, it will not be now that I die for death hath surely taken me already. He is gone, and I will go too, whether now or later or before or after, I will go all the same. If I were to have died, it would be no different than if I were to die now at this very moment, for everything after death is but nothing at all. I will never see him again, but truly it is as if I had never seen him at all, and him never I. I look down at my arm to see the hairs burning a soft glow. My legs no longer visible, the hall - which is no longer a hall at all, rather a soft, delicate blanket of fire - I see through my peripherals, and through my eyes, my true eyes, I see myself. At some point a mirror had descended directly in front of me, or perhaps it had been there all along, it made no difference. I see myself. It is not a great sight, but I cannot help but notice I no longer appear as I did. Once, I was who I was, and now in the mirror I am who I never was - who I am destined to be now and forever. My skin sags and I do not know if the fire melts my skin, or if it merely appears to do so. It has been so long since I peered into the surface of a mirror.

Oh how old I have gotten,
Oh how the fire has consumed me,
and now I is the only thing I have left.
There in the fire,
staring in the mirror
I wait
I wait for a return that will never come,
a day when I can be who I was,
I wait for something to happen to me,
a day when I can be who I am,
I wait too much and never enough,
Yet I must wait all the same,
here in the fire
melting in my everlasting reflection
bound to this hall in life and death,
waiting for one
or both
or none
Oh what have I done
but nothing at all?
So I close my eyes once more

and wish I was never to fall

March 17 or The Last Day I Recall

I wipe the drops from my eye lids as more take their place. The rain is quick but light and I do not feel wet from its presence. It is not dark out either for the sun shines through the clouds, its rays blocked by their gray fortress but felt through their slight transparency. I stand out in the field, my shoes sinking in the damp grassy moss that covers the bottom of this hill, as I stare at yet another gray surface. A large rock. Well, not very large but large enough to disrupt the greenery. I hated placing it here, it deserves a home among its own, but where else would it go? The downpour causes the stone to turn a darker shade and a pool to form at its base. The pool is just slightly red from the clay soil and trickles off further down the hill into the pond I call a pond, but really is just a permanent puddle that happens to house a frog I named Willie. I stand here waiting for something to happen, but nothing ever does. The rain simply pours and my feet sink a little lower.

I put my forearm to my brow so I can read the words of the stone. I already know what they say, I read them here every morning over the last forever that has passed, and every evening when the words, like a brand, sear their voice into my brain - in the space between my eyes and that which lies behind. The words, so bold, so effervescent, sit permanently in that space. Whenever they appear, I can never escape them, yet when I search for them, they slip away like dust in the wind,

79

like wisps in the air. So, I stand out in the field with my shoes sinking in the ever damp mesh of greenery to look at the words, ensuring they rest on the rock as I know they do and allowing my lips to hear their voice. The words speak to me as if I am not the one reading them aloud. The words come out of my mouth as if they are part of my breath. The words speak and I read them so I do not forget the ever present phrase. Oh how I scorn their unforgottenness. If only I could be free, if only I could forget and be.

I turn away from the rock and begin the moist march back up the hill. I really should dig out a trail one of these days. It rains so often it would do me well, but I can hardly find the motivation to do much of anything other than think of words nowadays. Words I wish I had spoken, words I wish had not existed, words I wish would never come, or would come sooner than never. Oh words… Of course I already forgot them, though not to worry! They will return to the space between my eyes and brain soon enough. I can almost see them, but to pine for them only dissolves their vague figure. My shoe slips and I catch myself with my hands. The grass is soft and lush and it does not hurt my hands. They are red now, slimy and slick. I look at my palms for a while as I walk. When I look up, I am staring at the face of my home, the reddish roof tiles more brown from the rain, the fading white exterior dripping and cracked, the single window clouded like the sky. I finally reach the rough dirt path and the rocks crunch under my soft, damp steps. I look just above my home, at the space where the roof meets the sky, so low I can almost reach it, and I see the edge of a dissipating cloud. The rays of the sun ever so slightly peer through, flowing over the tiles like the stream that flows to Willie's pond. If only it were not so lonely here at the edge of the hill, the house is beautiful and grand and goes to waste all just for I.

It happens often that I cannot enter. I stand outside on the rough dirt path staring at my home, maybe wishing it was the rock, maybe wishing it was someone, or some thing that could make me feel whole. But it is just a place, certainly no thing, not the thing. I feel paralyzed in these moments, like I am no longer controlling myself, like I no longer am myself. Rather, I see from some pair of eyes in the distance, some eyes that can see from nowhere eyes should be; yet, I see through them all the same. I see myself standing on the path, but I do not see my body, I see through myself into myself. I see what could not be seen by my eyes which only ever see out. I see in and without. Here the words have no power. They could be in my head all the same, but I cannot see them, for these eyes are not mine. To see through these eyes is all I ever wished for, but now I know they are eyes all the same. No matter who I am, I am always me, unfortunately.

At some point my vision returned, though it had never left, simply transferred from place to place, from eyes to mind and mind to eyes. I did not notice, however, for all I see is the words. The words I wish I knew how to read, though I could never. I do not know what they mean, but it is not the meaning of words that gives them power - what else are words other than spoken feelings? I feel the words inside me.

"Oh! How happiness courts the light, yet misery hides aloof," I cry out, "what have they done but make me be who I am?"

I do not want to be me, I simply want to be. However, that choice is not mine, I appear as I, and others see me as myself. But why me? Why must I be some one, why can I not be? I feel the words inside me once more, perhaps they had never left, my cries a failed attempt to scare them away.

"Oh to live! Oh humanity!" I scream this time, so rashly my throat is filled with needles and my chest rumbles. I fall to my knees but there is no comfort other than the words. The words. Please, please oh words escape me. I can no longer speak for all that comes out are the words. Over and over, the words, the words as if they are the only words. I mumble them to myself as I fall to the ground, my face in the rocks and my lips embracing the wet crumbles. I feel the words in the soil, the rocks spelling them out like braille to my lips. I do not have the energy to lift myself anymore, so I lay face down on the rough dirt path leading up to my home which I will never enter again. I intend to lay here forever, and never again after now. Although it is not my choice, it is certainly mine all the same.

I manage to eke out what I thought was my final word, yet it was not the single word I desired to utter. Instead, it was the words. It was always the words, could never be anything other than the words. I am the words, and the words are me forever and now. Oh the words! So, my final word was in fact two words and a letter, THE words. Oh how they escape me even now. I feel as if I could only remember them, maybe I could live. Maybe, just maybe, I could be. I do not remember them; how I wish for the rock, how I wish for the ability to read the words with my own eyes. A single drop of rain hits my right ear and runs down the side of my neck. I close my eyes and instead of eternal darkness, the kind of darkness one can never see, I read the words one final time, and forever:

Tyrannos x Basileus

www.ingramcontent.com/pod-product-compliance
Lightning Source LLC
Chambersburg PA
CBHW070349130626
46556CB00007B/3103